F

LAMB

The mexican

LARGE PRINT   £8.50

L 5/9

THE MEXICAN

Pablo Ortiz was a cheerful, hard-working *remudero* — until the day his Patron's daughter falsely accused him of molesting her. Hounded, whipped and left for dead by her irate father, the young Mexican, with the help of Pedro Gomez, leaves Mexico vowing one day to return and clear his name. But there were dangers to be faced, and Pablo suffered a baptism of fire. Always, though, his grim determination pulled him through until he could exact a deadly revenge.

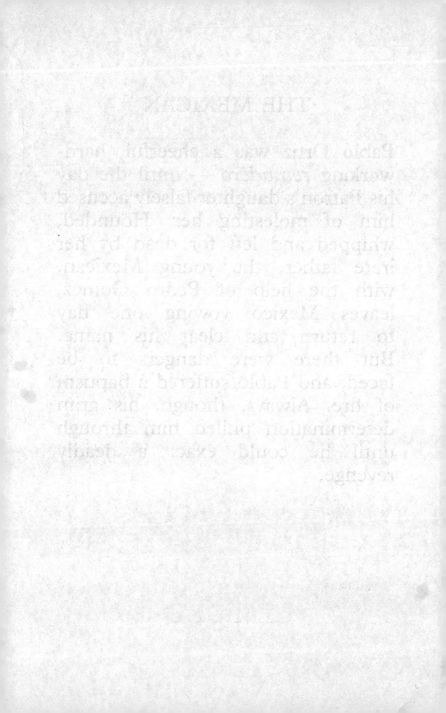

HAROLD LAMB

THE MEXICAN

Complete and Unabridged

LINFORD
Leicester

First published in Great Britain in 1998 by
Robert Hale Limited
London

First Linford Edition
published 1999
by arrangement with
Robert Hale Limited
London

British Library CIP Data

Lamb, Harold, *1929* –
    The mexican.—Large print ed.—
    Linford western library
    1. Western stories
    2. Large type books
    I. Title
    823.9′14 [F]

    ISBN 0–7089–5619–X

Published by
F. A. Thorpe (Publishing) Ltd.
Anstey, Leicestershire

Set by Words & Graphics Ltd.
Anstey, Leicestershire
Printed and bound in Great Britain by
T. J. International Ltd., Padstow, Cornwall

This book is printed on acid-free paper

1

The powerfully muscled legs of Pablo Ortiz pounded the sandy earth. His breath came in great gulps and his chest heaved as his sweat-glistened arms pumped across his body, urging his legs to go even faster. He heard the sound of the baying hound as it grew relentlessly nearer. Behind the hound, the drumming hooves of horses, accompanied by their riders' urgent voices, mixed with the barking of the hound.

Suddenly the hunted Mexican's ankle gave way on the rocky surface. He stumbled and staggered to recover his balance as the hound leapt at him, knocking him to the ground. Young Pablo Ortiz turned as he fell, his hand raised to grab at the slavering jaws. His strong fingers clamped round the pointed muzzle, keeping the jaws

1

tightly closed as they reached for his throat. The following horses pulled up as he struggled with the beast. The flamboyantly dressed leader of the riders dismounted and, gripping the hound by the scruff of its neck, pulled it from the fallen man. In his free hand, he held a whip, which he crashed across the hound's back as he flung it away from the quarry. The chastised animal stood off whimpering and growling.

'*Silencio, Raz*,' the man with the whip ordered and the dog crouched down, obedient to the stern command. Then the rider turned to the prostrate form of the Mexican, who lay panting on the ground. The whip rose and fell again, this time lashing down onto the defenceless body of the youth. Pablo Ortiz scrabbled over onto his hands and knees as he tried to escape the whip that was directed at him. As the stinging lashes began to cut into his back, he fell sprawling on his front, to be kicked mercilessly on the side of his body The breath left his lungs and the whip lashed him again and again. The young Mexican's fingers dug into the gritty earth. He bit his lower lip against the pain. The whip continued biting into his back. Then the pain was replaced by numbness and his body finally relaxed as he drifted into unconsciousness.

'*Patron*, I think he is dead,' one of the other riders said quietly. The whipping stopped and the speaker dismounted to inspect the body.

Don Felipe Lopez stood sweating and panting above the still, blooded figure, whose torn shirt flapped innocuously in the evening breeze.

With a curt nod to his *patron*, the kneeling *vaquero*, who was Don Felipe's *caporal*, stood up and waited for further instructions. The man with the whip slowly coiled it then kicked the body and spat on it, before walking to his horse.

'Come, Raz,' the well-dressed *hacendado* called to his hound as he hooked the whip back on his ornate saddle. He bent down to stroke the hound before mounting his horse.

'*Vamos*, let's go. Our work is finished here,' the ranch owner called to his *vaqueros* as he rowelled his golden palomino into a flying start. His workers swung their horses round and prepared to follow. Caporal Pedro Gomez remounted and blessed himself with the sign of the cross as he looked back at the prostrate form of young Ortiz. He hoped he was not dead. He had tried to save him further injury by lying to his *patron*, for he had no doubt that Don Felipe meant to kill the young man in his fury. Pedro Gomez knew Ortiz had not deserved the beating he had received, much less to die, but if you worked for Don Felipe Lopez you obeyed orders no matter what they were.

The pace of the riders slackened as they made their final approach into the valley. Don Felipe sat high in the saddle, not speaking till they entered the environs of the *hacienda*. The lights were still on in the main house. Don Felipe dismounted in the cobbled courtyard and tossed the reins to his *caporal*.

'Unsaddle him then go back and bury that *maldito* Ortiz.' Don Felipe walked slowly, with a heavy tread, towards the house. Gomez could sense a certain sadness in his *patron*. Now his temper had abated perhaps he was feeling some remorse. Ortiz, the young man, would be sorely missed. He had been good with the horses; a good *remudero*.

The door shut on Don Felipe. The *vaqueros* dismounted and Pedro Gomez handed the reins of his *patron*'s horse to one of them. 'See to him well, Manuel. I will go back to bury Ortiz.' The *caporal*'s voice was thick with emotion. The man who should have been attending to the horses was possibly lying dead by now. If that was so, then his *caporal* would bury him, but if by some miracle he was still alive, Pedro Gomez would help him to get away from the wrath of Don Felipe Lopez.

Gomez led a fresh horse out of the stables and mounted up. Tied onto the back of his saddle were canteens of water, bundles of clothing, food and a spade. In his pocket were a few silver coins. He noticed the curtains of one of the rooms of the main building move as he clattered over the cobblestones. He could see the outline of Señorita Maria Lopez. She was watching him ride away. He wondered how she felt, for it was she who had been responsible for what had happened to Ortiz.

He picked up speed as he left the *hacienda* and set a steady pace as he left the valley. His thoughts went back to the time when he had first met the young Mexican.

* * *

Ortiz had ridden into the yard on the back of a mule, looking for work.

Gomez could picture him clearly; dressed in ragged, off-white clothing, his long hair tied back by a red headband under a battered straw hat and an old pistol jammed in his waistband.

The barefoot young stranger had dismounted and was standing listening to Pedro Gomez who was shouting orders to a man who came to the door of the stables with a broom in his hands. Gomez had hold of the reins of a fine chestnut stallion and was telling the recalcitrant *remudero* that the horse and saddle were not up to scratch, before handing over the chestnut to be tended afresh.

'Do your job properly or you leave,' Gomez grated. The man took the beast lazily, muttering obscenities. The *caporal* turned on his heels in anger to be greeted by a smiling young Mexican stranger standing by a mule.

'*Señor Caporal*, I hear you say you are wanting a man who can look after horses.' Ortiz's smile broadened,

7

his even white teeth flashed, his eyes blue and sparkling with humour in his strikingly handsome face.

'I am that man, *señor*.' He bowed. 'Pablo Ortiz, *Señor Caporal*.'

Gomez studied the ragged but clean figure, the stocky, muscled build. His gaze turned to the mule. The animal stood sturdy and clean; its hide shone, it was evidently well looked after. Gomez bit his tongue to stop himself from dismissing the ragged rider.

'You are a *remudero*?' he questioned.

'I am anything you want me to be, *señor*.'

The stableman ambled from the stable, the chestnut walking with him.

'I have done the job.' he growled.

Gomez turned his attention from Ortiz to the stablehand and the chestnut. He could see no improvement in the animal's condition. Gomez turned to the young Mexican.

'You can start work now,' he said.

'Pablo Ortiz will not let you down, *señor*.' The ragged figure bowed as he spoke to the ranch *caporal*. Gomez spun round to face the stableman.

'Go, get your things. I'll get what's owing to you.'

The man cursed afresh and swung a punch at Gomez, catching him on the side of the head. The ragged figure moved with amazing speed. He jumped between the stableman and the *caporal* and pushed the man back as he went to kick Gomez, who was struggling to rise. The stablehand staggered back before throwing a punch at Ortiz who dodged the blow easily and threw one of his own. It crashed into the man's face, dropping him to the ground where he stayed immobile. Then Gomez found himself being helped to his feet by the ragged young man.

The *caporal* smiled as he thought of his introduction to Pablo Ortiz, who had turned out to be an exceptionally hardworking *remudero* as well as an excellent rider. He rode for Don Felipe, winning many races at local fiestas. Under his care, the don's livestock had improved and his horses sold for high prices thanks to the work of Pablo Ortiz. Now it would end thanks to Maria Lopez, the daughter of his *patron*, Don Felipe.

Gomez cursed her as he rode into the cold night, his eyes searching for the body of the young *remudero*. The howl of wolves echoed out in the night as they signalled their whereabouts to one another. He pulled his rifle from the saddle boot. His heels thumped his horse's side, hurrying it along once more, for he knew that if the wolves found Ortiz before he did there would not be much left to bury. Nearing the place where Ortiz had fallen, two wolves loped into view.

Gomez fired in their direction. One yelped and fell and the other hastily departed. The *caporal* knew it would come back to feast off its fallen companion, later.

Gomez did not have to search the area for long before he found the still, crumpled form of Pablo Ortiz. Jumping from his horse, he snatched a canteen of water and ran to the body and gently eased it over on to its side, causing the young Mexican to let out a moan. Gomez sighed with relief.

'*Gracias a Dios*. You are still alive, my friend,' he whispered as he tried, without success, to pour water between Ortiz's lips. Manoeuvring the unconscious youth so that he cradled his shoulders, Gomez sluiced his face with the water before laying him gently face down, with his head to one side. He examined the torn, blood-congealed shirt. Strips of cotton were sticking to the wounds, which were still seeping. Ortiz groaned again as the *caporal* carefully removed the ragged remains from his back with a dampened piece of cloth and bathed the lash wounds. The cuts and welts felt deep to the *caporal*'s fingers. Gomez shook his head. The don had used his full strength as he had whipped Ortiz.

Gomez could hear the burgeoning sound of wolves as they came ever closer. The smell of human blood was a big attraction. Laying the wet cloth across Ortiz's seeping back, he reached for his carbine and fired as one wolf, braver than the rest, came nearer. It bolted away.

The sound of the shot and the effects of the cold water broke into the unconscious mind of Ortiz. Slowly he moved his head and moaned again. His eyes tried to focus. He could feel hands on his face and cold water oozing from the rag pressed to his lips.

'It is I, Pedro Gomez,' the *caporal* assured Ortiz.

As the young Mexican tried to move, the pain from his back bit deep into him. He groaned as his senses began to swim again. Ortiz fought to stay awake. He felt Gomez's ministrations as the older man returned to his task. The water was soothing in its coldness but painful.

Ortiz recognized the voice speaking to him. It was *Señor Caporal* who gently turned him over and poured water into his mouth. He gulped and coughed and stifled a cry of pain as he fought to sit up. Gomez waited before proffering the canteen again. Ortiz gulped down the water. Feeling better he moved his head and the water ran down his front.

'I didn't touch her, *Señor Caporal*,' he whispered. A damp cloth wiped his face.

'I know you did not do this thing,' Gomez replied.

Slowly Ortiz manoeuvred himself into a more comfortable position to enable Gomez to gently apply some salve to his wounds. His back stung unmercifully, but he gritted his teeth and tried not to flinch. Covering the salve with a piece of clean cloth, Gomez helped Ortiz to his feet. The youth caught his breath as the effort jarred his aching ribs.

The *caporal* took a bundle from his saddle and, unrolling it, handed Ortiz an undershirt, a loose top, and a leather jacket to put on. Once dressed, Ortiz stiffly took a few steps, swayed and regained his balance.

'I see you are still very weak, my friend, but you must get away from here. There is a little money in the pocket of the jacket. It may help you,' Gomez said, leading Ortiz towards his horse.

In the distance, the howl of wolves echoed out again.

'Come, be strong. You can ride behind me.' The *caporal* climbed aboard his animal and reached out to haul the young *remudero* up behind him.

'I will take you to the border town. There you must stay and never come back this way, my young friend, for if you do Don Felipe will have you killed.'

'I did not touch Señorita Maria. It was she who came to me. Why should I run?'

The *caporal* did not reply. He had secretly witnessed what had happened but his allegiance, and his total dependence, was to his *hacendado*, Don Felipe. They rode in silence through the night, with Ortiz slumped against the back of his rescuer.

Ten miles on, Gomez reined in and waited while Ortiz lowered himself stiffly from the horse. Taking his Colt. 45 from his holster he handed it down to the waiting youth.

'You may need this,' he said, 'It is better than that old *pistola* I have seen you practising with.'

With a grateful nod, Ortiz placed it in his waistband.

'There is a gringo town called Riverville ahead,' the *caporal* said, pointing in the distance. 'It will be safe for you to stay there till you are well enough to move on. *Vaya con Dios*, my friend.'

The two men shook hands and Gomez swung his horse around and rode off without looking back.

Pablo Ortiz watched him disappear. The cold of the night stung his face and his clothes stuck to and dragged at his wounds as he shivered. He needed to keep on the move, he chided himself. Walking slowly and weakly he set off in the direction of the gringo town, stopping occasionally to ease the pain of his ribs and back.

Arriving at Riverville, Ortiz cautiously began to circle the perimeter of the town. The smell of horses came from a large building on the north side. He paused and looked around before entering the stable. He eased through the door and found an empty stall. Curling up in a corner, he closed his eyes. The smells and feel of the stable brought back the memory of the start of his troubles.

The fiesta had ended, the race had been won and the family of Don Felipe Lopez had returned in good spirits to the *hacienda*. Ortiz's last job had been to tend to Señorita Maria's horse. After rubbing it down and giving it a bucket of oats, he polished the saddle, hung it up and walked to the stable door for a breath of fresh night air. The

16

moon and stars were clear and bright in the cloudless sky. He breathed deep; the clean, sharp air swelling his lungs and chest. He was a lucky man; happy with his work and his life. The *patron*, Don Felipe was pleased with his work. His horse string was known throughout the area. Pablo Ortiz was a good *remudero* and an expert horseman. He had ridden for the *patron* and proved his horsemanship, winning many races for the Lopez family.

'Hello, Pablo.'

The young Mexican started from his reverie and turned as he heard his name whispered. The daughter of Don Felipe was close to him. He removed his straw hat which he always wore.

'*Señorita*?' He stood transfixed and nervously looked about. Nobody was afoot. The lights were on in the big house. Maria Lopez moved closer to the handsome *remudero*, who backed away into the stable.

'You did well in the race today,' she said.

'Thank you, Señorita Maria.'

She laughed and mimicked his subservient tone as she reached out and touched his arm. Then she pushed herself against him and kissed him. Shocked at her behaviour he stumbled back away from the girl. What was she doing? Then she came forward again laughing at his fear and tried to kiss him again. It was then that Don Felipe's voice called out her name. The *hacendado* was striding across the yard from the house in their direction. He saw his daughter being handled by somebody. It was then that Pablo Ortiz received a worse shock. Maria Lopez screamed and lashed out, her hand striking him across the face.

'Father, this animal, he tried to touch me.'

Don Felipe hurried towards his daughter who fell into his arms and broke down in hysterical tears. Ortiz did not stay to reason things out. He took to his heels and ran and ran, only to be caught and severely punished.

The only other person who could have told Don Felipe the truth was riding back to the *hacienda*. The *caporal* had witnessed the girl's actions while standing in the shadows of the building, but it would have been unwise even to infer disgrace on the daughter of a great *hacendado* such as Don Felipe Lopez. Pedro Gomez's own livelihood depended on his loyalty to his *patron* so the injustice of the punishment was accepted by the *caporal*, but the severity of it merited his assistance to the young Mexican who had once come to his aid on the day they had first met those many seasons ago. He had done what honour dictated he had to do for the young *remudero*. Now his debt to Pablo Ortiz had been repaid.

Pedro Gomez, *caporal* for *hacendado* Don Felipe Lopez, straightened his back, jutted out his jaw and flicked his horse into a gallop as he swung into the valley and down towards the *hacienda*.

2

Bill Jenkins, the owner of Riverville's livery stables rose early from his bunk. He rubbed his sparse, grey whiskers in agitation; partly because he had lost money to those thieving, so-called friends of his in the card game last night and partly because with the dawn came the knowledge that he was once again left on his own to see to the stables now his latest helper had up roots and gone.

'Helper, bah. Fickle no-good,' he muttered to himself as he raked at the old pot stove. He tossed in a few bits of kindling before replacing the replenished coffee pot. It would be ready by the time he had swilled his face in the water barrel outside.

As he passed one of the stalls, a pair of boots poked out from the straw piled at the back. He stared at them for a second before picking up a pitchfork to slap the boots with the pole end.

'Hey, what's going on here? This ain't no doss house.'

The straw parted and Pablo Ortiz, clawing the straw from his head and face, looked up sleepily at the ostler.

'A damn Mex,' the stable owner gasped, turning the steel prongs threateningly towards the youth. 'Get up and get out. I don't allow no greasers in here.' The young Mexican sat up awkwardly with a grimace and the ostler backed off slowly and studied the youth. It was evident that something wasn't right. He lowered the fork. He wasn't sure if the Mexican was pretending, but the grimacing looked real enough.

'For a young 'un you sure move old. What happened to you?'

Pablo Ortiz shook his head, 'It is nothing, *señor*. I needed somewhere to rest. If you will let me stay here for a while longer I will work to pay for the time I spend here.'

Old Bill Jenkins thought for a

minute. He certainly could use a bit of help and Mexican workers — if you could abide 'em — came cheap.

'You still haven't told me what you're doing in my stables. I don't want no business with anybody that brings trouble in their wake.'

The expression on the young Mexican's face changed from anxiety to sadness.

'Well, I guess that can wait a spell. A cup of coffee should help jog your memory and loosen your tongue.'

Heaving on the side rail, Ortiz pulled himself awkwardly to his feet. Bill Jenkins could see that the stranger was a well-muscled youth. It was then that he noticed the Colt stuck in the young man's waistband.

'And that there gun spells trouble,' he said raising the fork and prodding the Mexican's chest with it.

'No, *señor*,' the youth gasped, holding his free hand high, in submission. 'Take it, it is yours.'

He stood still as a statue as the old man stepped warily to his side and retrieved the Colt.

'Now march yourself in back. My coffee pot'll be boilin' over by now,' the ostler ordered, keeping a wary eye on his captive. Had the Mexican stopped a bullet, Bill Jenkins wondered, as the youth made his way haltingly ahead of him to the back room. He could see no obvious evidence of it but there was something amiss.

'What exactly's wrong with you? Are you able to work?'

Pablo Ortiz nodded. 'I can work, *Señor*. Soon I will be well and you will see.'

The coffee pot was sizzling away. Jenkins stuffed the Colt in his belt and, pouring two cups of the steaming liquid, handed one to Ortiz. He noticed him wince again as he sat down.

'Something's sure not right with you, boy. Reckon you'd better come clean if we're to get along. What's wrong with you?' he asked and watched as the youth finished drinking before deigning to answer. Had somebody in town beat up on him? Had he been caught stealing? He had no facial bruises that the old man could see.

'It's my back, *Señor*.'

'Then take your jacket off. Let's see what your trouble is.'

The Mexican hesitated for a moment, but seeing that the livery owner was determined, he struggled to remove his jacket. Bill Jenkins took hold of the jacket and waited while Ortiz removed his shirt and undervest. A bloodstained cloth fell to the floor. The old man gasped at the extent of the damage to the young Mexican's back. The bruises, welts and cuts were angry and needed attention

'Who the hell did that to you, boy?'

'My *patron*, Don Felipe Lopez, *señor*.'

'Why? Did you steal something?'

'No, *señor*, I did nothing.'

Slowly Pablo Ortiz told his story; how he had been wrongly accused and what the results had been and how he had been helped to escape by his *caporal*, Pedro Gomez.

'Why didn't you stay and deny it?' Jenkins asked him.

'You do not call your *patron's* daughter a liar, *señor*. That's why I ran.'

Jenkins shook his head in disbelief. He looked at Ortiz. He was a handsome boy. He could see why the girl had made a play for him.

'Stay sat,' he said. He went into the stable and came out with a bottle.

'Get over,' he said, easing the Mexican forward. 'This will sting a bit but it will help heal you.'

He poured the pungent liquid into his calloused hand and, as gently as he could, he rubbed it into the cuts. Ortiz cringed and gasped as the potion was applied. When the liquid covered his back, Jenkins corked the bottle. 'If it's good enough for the horses it'll be good enough for you,' he remarked, chuckling at his own joke. As Ortiz reached for his shirt, the livery owner stopped him.

'Leave it bare for now, you won't be going anywhere. The lotion will help dry the cuts. Now let's see what you know about cleaning out stables and looking after horses.' He tossed the pitchfork to Ortiz before turning his attention to the stove and his supplies. 'Start cleaning. I'll call you when the food's ready.'

With that he set to to cook some bacon with a few eggs. Pablo Ortiz took the fork and started work. Stopping only to eat the welcome food, the young Mexican was soon into a routine. There were a number of stalls which needed cleaning out and a couple of horses which needed tending to and rubbing down. His back injuries hindered him somewhat, but as the day went on, Bill Jenkins knew that he had hired good cheap labour.

During the next few days, with Jenkins's ministrations and the fact that the Mexican was young and healthy, Ortiz's wounds and his labour improved. He became less nervous of strangers once he was able to wear his shirt again, though he still declined to venture about the town preferring to stay based at the stables. For his part, Bill Jenkins had developed sufficient confidence and trust in his new hand to leave him in charge when he went out.

It was late one afternoon when the livery door opened and a tall, well-dressed man, leading a big chestnut horse, came in. He called out for attention as he took off his hat and started dusting down his suit with it. Pablo Ortiz came out of one of the stalls.

'*Si, señor?*'

The tall man studied the young Mexican.

'Where's the ostler in charge?'

'He will be back soon. I work here for Señor Jenkins.'

The stranger gave the place the once-over. It was certainly a clean stable block. He passed over the reins of his mount to the young Mexican. 'Take care of him and watch out, if you treat him wrong he'll let you know.'

Pablo took the reins. It was a good piece of horse-flesh. 'I will take good care of him, *señor.*'

The tall man tossed him a coin, 'That's for you. Where do I get a decent meal and a clean bed?' he asked.

'I do not know, *señor.* My work is here,' Ortiz replied.

The tall man looked at the young Mexican. 'OK, then. If you want me, concerning my horse, I'll be in the nearest saloon. Just ask for Lee Brent.'

Pablo Ortiz pocketed the coin. '*Si,* Señor Brent.'

The stranger left the stable and entered the first café he came to. Over his shoulder he carried a well-stocked saddle-bag. He saw that the place was clean and the food smelt good. Putting his saddle-bag on the floor by the table, he sat down, ignoring the stares of the customers who were already dining there. He adjusted his coat and settled his shoulder holster under his left arm before looking around for some service.

A middle-aged man came from behind the counter. 'Yes sir, what would you like?' The man was bald, red-faced and smiling.

'Steak and fries, please, and a coffee right away,' Brent said.

Pete, the owner, nodded and vanished into the back. In no time at all he reappeared with a mug of coffee and a homely, bonny woman peered around the doorway to note which table he served. She came to the door again when Pete served the stranger his meal and watched for a while as Lee Brent began to eat.

The food was good, he ruminated, as he sipped another mug of coffee, and decided he would eat here on a regular basis for as long as his visit lasted. Having satisfied his hunger, he called over to the middle-aged man for his bill.

'You've got a mighty fine cook back there,' he grinned. 'I'll be back again.'

'Thanks, mister. I'll tell the wife. Will you be staying in town long?'

'For a while, I reckon. I'm new to Riverville. Can you recommend a place to stay?'

'You can stay here. We have a spare room. I'll check with Martha.'

Pete went into the back to reappear with his wife. 'That's OK. My name's Pete and this here's Martha.'

'Lee Brent, ma'am. You sure are a good cook. Haven't tasted steak like yours for ages.'

Martha smiled. 'The room's at the back if you'd like to come through. The charge is two dollars a night. Meals and laundering will come extra. There's a side door you can use to come and go.'

Lee Brent agreed without haggling over the tariff. At the moment, money was not a problem. He picked up his saddle-bag and followed Martha as she bustled off to show him the room. He was pleased at the cleanliness of the place. He passed over his washing and twenty dollars saying, 'When you want extra, let me know.'

After a bath and a haircut, he walked to the Sunrise Saloon. Above the door it said, Mick Boyd, Proprietor. He entered and studied the place and its clientele. He looked across at the gambling tables. Three men sat at one, playing. He went to the bar and bought a whiskey before making his way over to the card table. Three pairs of eyes looked up at his tall frame.

'Is there room for another player?' he asked. The three players nodded as one. One of them eased out a chair, 'Sit down.' He held out his hand. 'Name's Myers, Doc Myers,' he said, going on to introduce the other two, 'This here's Buck Ellis — owns the store — and the other old-timer is Bill Jenkins — he owns the livery stables.'

Lee Brent introduced himself as he shook hands. 'I left my horse over at your stables,' he said to Jenkins. 'And your helper hasn't come running for me. I take it that's a good sign.'

The ostler agreed. 'Yes sir, your horse is in good hands.'

Doc Myers grinned and slapped the ostler on the back. 'You've never had it so good, have you, Bill?'

Jenkins picked up his cards. 'Let's play,' he growled. 'Poker. Highest deals.'

The others nodded. Doc Myers won the right to deal. Two hours later, the three friends had lost ten dollars each. The stranger seemed to know what they had even when they dealt themselves. The four players left the Sunrise Saloon together, having agreed to meet again the following day.

Lee Brent left them talking outside and made his way over to the stables to check on his mount before turning in. He found his horse well groomed and settled. Turning to leave, he was surprised to find he was not alone. Instinctively Brent's hand reached under his armpit for his concealed Navy Colt.

'Oh, it's you,' he exclaimed, identifying the stocky form of Pablo Ortiz. 'I didn't hear you approach.'

Ortiz showed neither fear nor surprise. He stood his ground, barefoot and steady.

'I heard a noise, *señor*. Is everything all right?'

'Yes. I was just checking on my horse. I will call in every night,' Lee Brent replied, and left the stables, passing the owner on his way out. 'Your boy's done a good job with my chestnut, Mister Jenkins. Goodnight,' he said, and walked along to the side door of Pete's Café that led directly to his room. He took the key from his pocket, opened the door and entered.

Bill Jenkins watched the newcomer stride away and, shaking his head, entered the stables and closed the door. Pablo Ortiz was still standing by the stall.

'Is that the stranger's horse?' Jenkins asked.

'*Si, patron.*'

33

'I'm not your *patron*. Don't call me that,' he told the young man as he looked over the chestnut. 'That's a good piece of horseflesh,' he said. 'Cost a fair amount of money I reckon and the likes of me helped to pay for it no doubt,' he growled. 'Dull the lamp and get some sleep,' he called back to Pablo as he went off to his own room at the back of the stables.

'Slippery cuss,' he muttered, pulling off his boots. 'I've never seen such luck.'

Thoughts of Lee Brent and the way he had read the card game gave way to dreams of winning back a fortune as the old man pulled the blanket over his spare frame and fell into a noisy sleep.

From his makeshift bed in the lofted area of the stables, Pablo Ortiz could hear the burgeoning snores and the noise brought him some comfort. For now, at least, he was safe, warm and well fed. He closed his eyes and a smile crossed his face before he dropped off to sleep.

* * *

Saturday night in the border town was a busy time, this weekend it would be doubly so. The crew of the Flying W spread was in town for its monthly jaunt; to drink and gamble and visit the whorehouse. Mick Boyd's saloon would be one of the busiest places. Old Bill Jenkins had decided to skip his usual visit to the card game and was sitting in his room, reading an old magazine Doc Myers had given him. He could hear Ortiz moving about in the stalls.

'Pablo,' he called out. The young man came into the room.

'*Si?*'

'Why don't you stretch your legs some? A young 'un like you needs to get out and take a look around town; get the feel of the place.'

'I will give it some thought, Señor Bill.'

The ostler did not push the lad and went back to his magazine.

Later he heard the door open and shut, then everything went quiet. He smiled. It would do Ortiz good to get out. It had been over a month since he had first met the young Mexican in the stall.

Pablo Ortiz decided that a stroll along the board-walks, up and down the main street, would give him a safe glimpse of Riverville's night-life. Tucked in his waistband was Pedro Gomez's Colt. 45 that Señor Bill Jenkins had returned to him. The youth buried his face down into the upturned lapels of his jacket. The semi-darkness, too, would help conceal the fact that he was Mexican and perhaps keep bullying gringos from targeting him. He felt in his waistband. The .45 gave him a kind of comfort. He knew he could use it but would he have the nerve to defend himself against a gringo? If he shot one he knew he would be hanged. He shuddered at the thought of it. His thoughts flipped back to Don Felipe and his escape from the *hacienda*.

So engrossed was he that he barely noticed the five horsemen who pulled up alongside of him. They dismounted and tossing their reins across the tie post outside the saloon pushed their way boisterously towards the bar-room doors as the young Mexican crossed their path. One of the crew of the Flying W cursed as the stocky figure balked his progress.

'Watch where you're going' he gritted and a heavy arm crashed across the head and shoulders of Pablo Ortiz causing him to stagger slightly to one side. The agitated cowboy lashed out again. This time Ortiz saw the fist swinging towards him and dodged the blow. The light from the saloon shone on his face.

'It's a Mex and you missed,' one of the others teased.

The cowboy's anger rose and he moved after the side-stepping Mexican, his fist clenched. He aimed another mighty swing. Missing again he aimed a kick. Pablo dodged again. He looked round for a way of escape but he was faced on all sides by the Flying W crew who continued to bait their companion. The gringo lost his temper completely and, standing upright, he pulled at his gun. It was a cumbersome draw. Pablo Ortiz froze on the spot.

Suddenly a gun exploded nearby and a bullet hit the boardwalk between the agitated crew-member's feet.

'Put that gun away or the next bullet won't be between your feet but between your eyes.'

The cowboy hesitated as he looked at the tall figure of Lee Brent. He stood with his pistol pointed steadily at the enraged cowhand's chest.

'Put that gun away. I won't tell you again,' he ordered. The hulking crewman hesitated a moment before holstering the gun. His four companions stood by not sure what to do and wondering how good the stranger was with his cocked Navy Colt.

At last one of them spoke, 'Come on, Al. Leave it be.' The big man lingered for a while before turning to face Ortiz.

'Stay clear of me, Mex,' he said, and without a glance at Brent he followed his companions into the saloon.

Lee Brent replaced his gun and stepped up beside the young Mexican.

'So you decided to come out. Allow me to buy you a drink?'

'No, *señor*, it is better that I make no more trouble for you.' He turned to make his way back to the stables.

'There won't be any trouble,' said Brent, taking hold of Pablo by the arm. 'Come on.'

Together, the gambler and the Mexican entered the saloon to be met with the glowering stare of the big hulking figure at the bar. The Flying W ramrod was determined to save his face in front of his crew.

'You going to nursemaid the little greaser?' he asked contemptuously of the tall gambler.

Before Brent could answer, young Ortiz responded to the range rider's bait. 'I do not need a nursemaid, *hombre*. Pablo Ortiz can fight for himself.'

The talk in the saloon ceased. The customers stared across to the bar.

Al Rowan, the ramrod of the Flying W, was known for his short temper.

Lee Brent hesitated. He did not want to demean his young companion. He stepped away and then addressed the four ranch hands. 'No matter what happens, you lot stay out of it.'

The ramrod looked at Pablo Ortiz who stood balanced on the balls of his feet. He had taken off his jacket and put it on the bar. Al Rowan could see the Colt .45 in his waistband. The ramrod smiled wryly. He was not a fast gun but he reckoned he could outdraw this Mexican.

The men standing close to him moved away from the line of fire. Rowan's hand rested near his gun. The young Mexican stood like a coiled spring, his eyes unwavering. Rowan felt a niggle of fear. He moved his hand away from his gun and started to undo the buckle of his gunbelt.

'I'd sooner fist fight you, Mex. That way I can beat you to a pulp.'

Pablo Ortiz relaxed for a moment. It was then that Al Rowan's hand switched back to his gun. After all it was only a greaser he was going to shoot, fair way or foul, it didn't matter. His hand was still resting on his gun when the young Mexican's hand blurred back to his waistband and suddenly Al Rowan was looking at a Colt .45 aimed straight at his midriff. His body tensed as he waited for the lead slug to burst into his innards. The crowd expected the Mexican to shoot. He had every reason to kill Al Rowan after the ramrod had tried to bluff him with the belt trick.

'Let it be, kid.' It was Lee Brent who broke the silence.

Keeping his eyes on the ramrod, Pablo Ortiz handed his gun to the gambler, 'I will fight him now, *señor*.'

Rowan released his breath. He had

been made to look a fool but now it was his time to turn the tables. He undid his belt and handed it with his gun to one of his crew.

The saloon crowd stepped further away from Pablo Ortiz and Al Rowan. Lee Brent looked round for the ramrod's companions. They stood on the edge of the crowd. He pointed the gun at them.

'Remember what I told you. Don't interfere,' he repeated. They nodded and moved further away. Lee Brent suddenly had an idea.

'Before they begin, do any of you want a bet on the outcome of the fight?' he asked, pulling a roll of notes out of his pocket. He liked the look of Pablo Ortiz — he was well built, his shoulders and arms well muscled. He stood solid and well balanced and Brent had seen him dodge the blows that Rowan had swung at him outside the saloon. Most of the crowd had seen Al Rowan perform in many a fracas and the ramrod had a reputation as a good roughhouse fighter. His crew took up the offer and this started a rush by the rest of the saloon clientele.

The saloon owner, Mick Boyd, took the bets and scribbled names frantically on a piece of paper. While this was being done, the chairs and tables were moved and a fair-sized space was made. The bar did good business — to Mick Boyd's satisfaction — and Lee Brent kept a weather eye on his protégé, Pablo Ortiz, while the crowd settled down to await the fight.

The town's livery owner had been alerted and he came puffing into the saloon to place his bet on his young employee before going to stand alongside the gambler.

'I reckon even if young Pablo don't beat Al Rowan he sure as hell will put up a good fight.'

Doc Myers agreed to be in charge of the proceedings and finally, Mick Boyd threatened banishment for life if anybody else got involved in the fight. The place went quiet.

Doc Myers shouted, 'Right, start,' and hurried out of the contestants' way.

Al Rowan edged forward, his big fists held out in front of him. He took a swing at Ortiz, who moved away with easy agility. The crowd drew in their breath simultaneously as the punch missed. If it had hit home the Mex would have landed across the border. Suddenly Pablo Ortiz darted forward. His fist tattooed on the face and head of Al Rowan bringing him up short. The crowd gasped at the force of the punches. One punch cracked the big bully's nose. A left swing cut Rowan's eye. A following right hand rocked the ramrod who staggered back, his hands lifting to protect his face. He was surprised at the strength of the punches and the speed of them. Ortiz moved in close to him now as he fell back against the bar. Then the blows were hitting him in the fleshy part of his belly. The young Mexican's fury increased. All his pent-up resentment at how he had been treated in the past welled up inside him, turning him into a battering machine. His lips twisted. He snarled and cursed in his native tongue. The young *remudero's* punches smashed again into Rowan's face as his hands dropped low to protect his belly. The blows ripped at his face and blood flowed freely from the many cuts. Somebody shouted. 'Stop the Mex,' as Al Rowan sank to his knees before falling face down on the saloon floor.

Doc Myers stepped into the circle and dragged at Ortiz's arm, pulling him away so that he could inspect the prostrate form.

'You've nearly killed him, young fellow,' he said. 'You're one hell of a fighter.'

Pablo Ortiz stood panting, the fury slowly leaving him.

'Help me get him up,' Doc Myers asked the silent, gaping crowd. Rowan's four companions came to his aid and the crowd began to discuss what they had just witnessed.

'Get me a bucket of warm water and a bottle of whiskey,' the doc called. 'And keep my winnings somewhere safe till I've fixed this fella up,' he added, addressing Mick Boyd as the bar owner paid out the winnings to the handful of men who had bet on the young Mexican.

Lee Brent took most of the pot and had to borrow a bag from Boyd to carry his loot. His poker game had been ruined, but he had made more in one evening than he usually made in a week.

Jenkins, the livery owner was also a happy man. He had won ten dollars.

Together they accompanied Pablo Ortiz outside and back to the stables.

'Where did you learn to fight like that?' the ostler asked Ortiz.

'In my village. You learn to fight to live.'

Lee Brent passed back his gun. 'Is that where you learnt to handle a gun?' he asked.

Pablo nodded, '*Si, señor*, but I have

never shot anybody.'

Lee Brent shook his head in disbelief. This Mexican was quite an unusual young man. The gambler was fast with a gun — in his profession he had to be — but this Ortiz was quicker, much quicker. The bag in his hand jingled. The gambler was pleased. He suddenly had an idea.

He would sleep on it. Tomorrow he would put his idea to Pablo Ortiz.

That night, Lee Brent decided he would sleep in the stables just in case Al Rowan or his crew decided to make a midnight call.

3

The next morning Jenkins's coffee pot was emptied a number of times. The smell of bacon was thick in the air as the three men finished their breakfast. Pablo Ortiz gathered up the plates and took them out back to rinse them.

'Might as well get it over with now,' the gambler stated, as he put down his coffee mug.

Jenkins stopped chewing as he waited to hear what Lee Brent had to say.

'I'm leaving today, old-timer.' The gambler rose and, retrieving the bag containing his winnings, he counted out thirty dollars on the table in front of Bill Jenkins, adding, 'I want to buy your best horse.'

The ostler was surprised at the request. The gambler had the big chestnut which was equal to any of Jenkins's stock. He asked Brent why he wanted another horse.

'I want it for young Pablo — that's if he wants to come with me. I have a proposition to put to him.'

Jenkins spluttered into his coffee. 'I don't want to lose him. He's the best helper I've ever had.'

Lee Brent held up his hand, silencing him. 'Just think about it. I don't think his stay here will be a pleasant one after the skirmish with Rowan last night. Anyway, let's put it to the young fella and see what he thinks.'

With that, Bill Jenkins hollered for the young Mexican and, once he was seated, Pablo Ortiz listened to Lee Brent's proposal. When the gambler had had his say the two men focused their attention on the youngster.

'*Señor*, I like working for Señor Jenkins. What work can you give me? You do not have many horses for me to look after.'

Lee Brent shook the bag and then tipped it on the floor of the livery stable. Ortiz's eyes rounded in surprise at the amount of money.

'That's what I won backing you last night.' Brent said.

'I, too, was a winner, Señor Jenkins. See, I won two dollars,' the beaming Mexican said, showing the coins that the gambler had given him. Lee Brent stooped down and picked up his money and replaced it into the bag.

'There is nothing stopping you from getting much more,' he told the young Mexican.

'I don't understand you, *Señor*.'

'Nor I,' said Jenkins.

Brent looked at the pair of them. 'I want Pablo to leave here and come with me. Together we can travel all over America — west and east — visiting all the big cities; New York, Chicago — fighting; fist-fighting. You have a lot of ability, young Pablo. I have seen many fighters — all shapes, all breeds, all styles — but I have never seen the likes of you. We can start off with the towns, mining camps and steamboats, up and down the rivers. I will supply the money. We will challenge any man to a fist fight and share the winnings equally.'

Jenkins shook his head in disbelief. 'Have you gone mad? You won a bit of money last night and it's turned your head. Look at him,' he commanded, nodding towards the young Mexican 'He ain't but middlin' in size and he ain't gonna grow no bigger. I've seen some of those fighters. They're giants.'

Jenkins's outburst was dismissed by Brent. 'I've seen them too, old-timer, all brawn and brute strength without a thought for their own well-being. Drinking and fighting, womanizing and boozing when the money's there, scrounging on their past glory when their time's running out. That won't happen to this young man. He's got something special and I'll look after him. We'll make enough money to retire on. Pablo will be able to buy his own horses, train them, race them . . .'

Jenkins waved his hands dismissively. 'I think you're mad, Mr Lee Brent,' he said. 'Anyway, it's up to the lad himself.' He tossed the dregs of coffee on the earth floor. Lee Brent stared at young Ortiz.

'What do you think? If it doesn't work out I will pay you off and you can find a job wrangling anywhere.'

The young Mexican was not listening to Brent's alternative. The thought of owning his own *hacienda* with his own horses sent his senses reeling.

'*Si, Señor*,' he whispered with fervour, 'I will go with you.'

★ ★ ★

Bill Jenkins stood at the livery door watching the two riders head out of town along the road that led to the Rio Grande and Tucson. That was the first town Lee Brent had said would be their destination. Jenkins thought of the fifty dollars the gambler had paid him for the big bay and saddle and other things the young Mexican needed. He should have been happy at such a generous payment, but somehow it felt to him like thirty pieces of silver. Jenkins spat and re-entered the building. He would miss the young Mexican who had made life easier and more companionable for the old ostler since his arrival. Jenkins picked up the pitchfork to toss some hay.

'Dammit,' he said, as he set about the daily chores with more than his usual vigour.

* * *

Lee Brent and Ortiz boarded the ferry and crossed the Rio Grande. The town of Tucson was ahead of them as they stepped onto solid ground. Brent was beginning to feel a bit apprehensive. He hoped he had not over-anticipated the young Mexican's capabilities in the excitement of the events in Riverville. Mulling it over, Brent reasoned that the youngster had enough power in his punching for a man twice his size and that, coupled with his phenomenal speed of delivery, put the odds in their favour. Having shaken off his doubts, the gambler urged both horses forward with a cheerful rally, 'Tucson, here we come.'

Tucson was a thriving place with new buildings being erected higgledy-piggledy on the approaches to the outskirts of town.

'Just smell that money, Pablo,' Lee Brent grinned, as they slowed their horses to a walk.

'I can smell only wood,' the young Mexican answered with a puzzled expression.

Neater rows of buildings had been erected edging the main road and the population there thickened as cowboys mixed with business folk and city gentry from the East.

As they rode down the main street, they passed the marshal's office. A man with a star on his vest and sporting a tied-down .45 on his right hip stood watching them ride in. After giving them the once-over, his eyes scanned past them to register other new arrivals who had come across on the ferry. His stare did nor falter; it took in everything and everybody.

Pablo Ortiz was doing the same thing. He was assessing the people and their possible reaction to him as he guided his horse skilfully through the bustling throng on the way to the livery stables at the far end of the main street.

The ostler took both beasts from them and the handful of coins Brent proffered, with a few precise instructions. Ortiz collected their saddle-bags while the gambler asked the ostler for the name of a good rooming-house.

'We'll dump our gear and find an eating-place,' Brent said. 'I bet you could eat a horse.'

'I'm too excited to eat, *Señor*,' Pablo replied.

'Then it's a good thing I'm looking out for you. A good fighter needs his vittles . . . regular,' retorted Brent.

Having dropped off their saddle-bags, they wandered out of the rooming-house to find a good eating-place. A café with a bright green façade caught the gambler's eye. 'Ryan's', a notice outside read. 'Try our Irish stew. The best in town.' Lee Brent led the way in. It was a busy place and the woman behind the counter was calling out orders, in a thick Irish brogue, to three girls who were cheerfully running between the tables. One of the waitresses, a pretty, dark-haired girl, came across to greet them and led the hungry travellers to an empty table and waited for them to be seated before asking for their order. Brent asked for the Irish stew and the young Mexican mumbled, '*Si, por favor, señorita*,' when the waitress asked if he wanted the same.

Pablo Ortiz blushed as she smiled and teased, 'For you and your friend, my handsome young *señor*, I will bring the best.'

Lee Brent grinned and scanned the clientele in the café before allowing his gaze to travel through the window to watch the people as they passed by, whilst they waited for their order. Pablo Ortiz sat still and quiet at the table, hardly daring to lift his eyes from the tablecloth in case they caught the mischievous glance of the pretty waitress. He found it all very exciting; the whole town, the hustle and bustle, and the people — especially the pretty . . . His thoughts were interrupted when two steaming bowls of Irish stew were placed on the table.

'I will bring your bread, *señor*,' the waitress said, as Pablo mumbled his thanks, and she hurried off to return with a plate of thick chunks of freshly baked bread.

'There you are, my fine fellow. Get yourself round that and you'll be fit for anything,' she laughed, with a wink directed boldly at the freshly blushing Mexican.

'You've made a good impression

there, Pablo,' Brent said.

'How, *señor?* I do not wish to cause any trouble.'

'Trouble?' Brent queried and then laughed. 'Aye, trouble. I reckon you're gonna cause enough of that before we leave Tucson . . . and get paid for it. Eat your stew.'

The stew was good and provided a filling, wholesome meal. Lee Brent pushed back his chair and searched in his vest pocket for his toothpick. The café had quietened down and the woman behind the counter left her post and made her way towards him. Lee Brent watched her as she made her slow, deliberate approach. She took in his appearance — the waistcoated suit, white shirt and string tie; the manicured hand that held the toothpick; the good looks and strong jaw.

A dude, she thought, and one who can take care of himself, I'll be bound. She studied his companion, the young Mexican. A strange pair of bedfellows, to be sure, she mused. A dude and his lackey, no doubt. A handsome lackey at that. Her face broke into a broad smile as she picked up their plates and asked, 'Did you enjoy your meal?'

'Sure did, ma'am, that's the best stew I've tasted in a long time.'

She nodded, proudly. 'Coffee? The fruit pie's good . . . I can recommend it.' She paused enquiringly.

'Pablo, can you manage a piece of pie?' Brent queried.

'*Si, señor . . . señora.*'

'That settles it then. Two pies, two coffees and, if you don't mind me asking, which saloon would you recommend?' the gambler asked.

'I don't mind you asking one bit,' the woman laughed. 'Gallagher's, opposite. It's owned by my brother.' She made her way back to her position behind the counter and, when the pies and coffee arrived, she detailed them off to the tables with the girls. The pie, blueberry and apple, went down well, followed, more leisurely, by the freshly brewed coffee. Lee Brent resumed his observations, focusing on the saloon across the road as he sipped the last of his coffee. Men were going in and out in an orderly fashion and if the café was anything to go by the saloon was probably just as well run. Pablo's fidgeting caught the gambler's attention. The young Mexican was ready to leave.

'Right, let's go, Pablo,' Brent said and, rising from his chair, Brent made his way to the counter where he settled the bill, while Pablo shuffled to the door and held it open waiting for his friend. Glancing over to the pretty waitress he blushed again as she winked and blew him a kiss. 'You really will have to do something about that face-pinkin' you're prone to,' Brent warned softly, as they left the premises.

Together they crossed the road to Gallagher's. It was a spacious saloon; noisy and busy. The gambling area was at the back of the building, beyond the dance floor with its circling of tables. Midway along, two men — with Winchester rifles cradled on their laps — sat on opposite sides of the saloon. A shotgun stood in a slotted holder by each of them. Both men constantly searched the saloon's long room for signs of trouble. Either side of the gambling area, ran a pair of staircases leading to a balustraded landing which sported six doorways. A long bar ran down one side of the saloon and an upright piano and tables fulfilled the requirements for the dancers and girls on the opposite wall. The girls who were on offer did not go near the gamblers. They sat at the tables curved around the dance-floor area.

Lee Brent motioned for Ortiz to take a seat near the piano player, who was playing a noisy, lively tune, before collecting a beer and proceeding to find himself a place at a gambling table where there was an empty chair. He was readily accepted by the rest of the players and was pleased to find that there was no limit in the game. This, he felt, was gonna be his kind of town.

The young Mexican sat self-consciously looking round. He felt out of place in the gringo's saloon. He was invited to dance by one of the saloon girls but he declined and their ensuing stares coupled with wooden glances by the gringo fraternity made him feel even more uneasy. Seeing another of the girls making her way towards him, Pablo Ortiz stood up and hurried over to Lee Brent and stood behind him with his back to the dance floor.

A big, heavily built man stepped from one of the rooms on the landing and called out a greeting to a sombrely dressed redheaded man who was entering the saloon as he descended the stairs. Joining him at the bar they both turned to survey the clientele as they engaged in conversation. Drinkers, dancers and gamblers acknowledged the big man as they came and went and his private conversation was interspersed with 'welcomes' and the minutiae of everyday comments which he readily entered into, for he was Tom Gallagher, the owner of the saloon. His private conversation completed, both men began to stroll between the tables, Gallagher giving his attention solely to his clientele. His speech was as colourful as his waistcoat as he paused to speak to his customers, in his thick Irish brogue. Tom Gallagher was a popular man; fair and honest. His companion was Pat Ryan — his brother-in-law and the saloon trouble-shooter.

Ryan was a well-made individual, if not quite as tall and broad as Gallagher, and sported a shock of red hair, long sideburns and a walrus moustache. His manner was less gregarious and his attire was less flamboyant, but if any fights started then he was the one to finish them. If guns were involved then the two gunhands sitting on each side of the room were ready to use their carbines or shotguns, but there were not many nights of trouble.

Tom Gallagher stopped at Brent's

table and nodded to the four gamblers. He studied Lee Brent as he picked up the pot he had just won before addressing Pablo Ortiz who stood alongside his friend.

'Are you waiting to join the game, m'boy?'

The Mexican shook his head. Brent butted in, 'He's with me.'

'With you is he? I hope he's not giving you signals,' Gallagher said affably.

'What kind of signals?' Brent asked.

'What cards the other players have. Those kind of signals,' Gallagher explained dryly. 'I see you have just taken a tidy pot.'

'He's not moved. How can he give signals if he doesn't move?'

The other three gamblers nodded in agreement, as Tom glanced from one to the other.

'Fair enough, but his presence could disturb the other players' concentration. Perhaps he'd like to pass the time, more pleasantly, with one of the girls while

64

you're playing cards?'

Brent's face broke into a smile, 'I don't think he'd know what to do with one. Anyway, he's in training.'

'For what? The priesthood?' Gallagher laughed.

'He's a fighter,' Brent explained.

'A fighter?' The Irishman's attitude changed to one of mild surprise and he studied the young Mexican more intently. He noted the Colt in his waistband.

'A gunfighter?' Gallagher suggested softly. 'Some kind of personal bodyguard, like Ryan here?'

'No, he's a fist-fighter.'

The saloon owner weighed up Pablo Ortiz.

'You're telling me you'd be prepared to bet on him winning fights?' he laughed. 'Do you think he can beat my man Ryan?'

Pat Ryan glanced scornfully at the young Mexican. He was taller by a good few inches and at least two stone heavier. He could not see the Mexican lasting five minutes with him.

'How much would you want to bet on your man beating Ryan here?' Gallagher continued.

'As much as I win tonight,' Brent replied. 'Will you shake on it?'

Without a second thought, Gallagher reached out, gripped Brent's extended hand and gave it a good shaking. 'See me before you leave,' he said. Ryan was laughing as the two Irishmen moved away.

Ortiz had heard the conversation between Brent and Gallagher. It looked as if his first fight was to be very soon. He wondered how much he would get for this fight. Up to now he had acquired a horse and saddle, food and a gun. Tonight he would talk to Lee Brent about the lump sum of money the gambler had said he would share with him.

4

Pablo Ortiz left Gallagher's saloon and made his way to his lodgings. He had felt out of place standing beside Lee Brent as the gambler continued playing late into the night. The young Mexican had hoped to talk to Lee Brent about the money that the gambler had promised him. Up to now, any money had come in small doses. The gambler had said he had made a lot of money from Pablo's fight with Al Rowan. Well, if Lee Brent wanted him to fight for money then Pablo wanted more than he was getting, for he was hoping one day to have enough money to buy his own ranch and fill it with horses. One day, the name of Pablo Ortiz would be famous as a horse-breeder. He would return to Mexico, where he would confront Don Felipe Lopez and tell him that his daughter had defamed his good name and that he, Pablo Ortiz, was not a molester of women.

The young Mexican fell asleep before Lee Brent returned. The gambler entered the room quietly and smiled as silently he made ready for bed. He had had a good night with the cards and now had over a thousand dollars to gamble on the fight. Gallagher had refused odds, preferring to cover dollar for dollar what Brent was prepared to put down. When he saw that the saloon-keeper could not be persuaded otherwise, Lee Brent had agreed. Gallagher was to arrange the date and venue with Ed Stewart, the town's marshal and would meet with the gambler at Ryan's café the following morning.

The next morning Brent and Ortiz ambled over to Ryan's café where Gallagher, Ryan and Marshal Ed Stewart were already waiting for them. The town lawman was introduced to the gambler and Ortiz as they joined the seated trio and sat down.

'So you're the fighter.' Stewart said, appraising the stocky Mexican, 'How many fights have you had?'

Pablo Ortiz was stuck for words. Lee Brent came to his aid. 'This will be his first,' the gambler answered. 'I found him in trouble, being harassed by a bully. He defended himself very well and here we are.'

'And you're his backer, I understand,' the marshal said, not showing any change in his expression.

'Señor Brent has been very good to me. I like to fight for Señor Brent,' Young Ortiz blurted enthusiastically.

'Well, if you're prepared to have a go, of your own free will, I don't see any problem,' the town marshal said, and turned his attention to details of venue and date.

'Have you any particular place in mind?' he asked Gallagher.

'How about the meadow, north of the town?' said the Irishman 'It's flat and level — ideal for a town gathering. We could make a date, say, two days from now — Sunday. We could charge a dollar entrance fee and share the money between us.'

The marshal pulled a face and tugged at his ear before speaking. 'Sunday's a tricky day, bein' church day and all . . .'

'But that's the only day we're sure to get a good crowd in town. The more people, the more money,' Gallagher interrupted.

Ed Stewart grinned at the Irishman. 'I'll put it to the town council. I'm sure half a share of the takings will help to persuade them.'

Gallagher rubbed his hands when Marshal Stewart left. 'Well, it looks like we have a fight on on our hands, boyo. Sunday it is then — if the council agree? He rose and, slapping the gambler on the back, said he would see him in the saloon later to discuss the council's decision. Ryan smirked at the young Mexican and whispered in his ear as he left the table. Ortiz's face flushed bright red and Brent laid a hand on his arm to keep him seated.

'Whatever he said, take no notice. He's just trying to jangle your nerves.'

'He said to enjoy my breakfast . . . '

'That's good advice. Take it,' Brent said, signalling to the waitress for attention.

'He said it would be my last . . . ' the young Mexican hissed between clenched teeth.

'He could be right. Your last breakfast in *this* town,' laughed Brent.

The dark-haired waitress was soon in attendance. After serving them, she hovered by the table.

'Is it right you are going to fight Patrick Ryan?' The young Mexican looked up from his plate and nodded.

'You must have a wish to be dead,' she said, 'You aren't even half his size. I'll have you know he was the bare-fist champion of Ireland.'

'You put your money on the Irishman then and I'll cover your bet,' Brent suggested calmly.

'It's all right for you: it's not your

71

life that's at stake,' she said, as she spun round and left the table.

The two men set to to enjoy their breakfast but were duly interrupted by the return of the young waitress with the woman from behind the counter, who was Ryan's wife.

She laughed loudly, when the waitress identified Pablo Ortiz as the fighter. 'Surely it not you Katherine says is to fight our Patrick?'

'*Si, señora*, it is I,' Ortiz said solemnly.

She turned her attention to Brent. 'Is this your harebrained idea? Have you got money to throw away? Because this fella has no chance of beating Patrick Ryan.'

The gambler finished his coffee before speaking. 'We think differently, don't we, Pablo? And if you have money to say different put it on your Irishman. It will be covered.'

'Señor Brent is right,' Pablo said. 'I will beat Señor Ryan.'

'You are both completely mad,' the

café-owner said, shaking her head in disbelief.

Brent smiled and rose from the table with Ortiz following suit.

'Much as we'd like to stay and continue this conversation, I'm afraid we must go. We will be back later for our evening meal. Have your money ready. I will be only too pleased to cover it.'

The café-owner shrugged her shoulders and returned to her post. Katherine, the waitress, watched them leave the café with a sense of foreboding. She had seen Ryan fight. Ortiz had no chance. She would see him later and try to talk him out of fighting Pat Ryan.

By the evening, the fight, date and venue had been agreed and confirmed by the town council and the town was buzzing with the prospect of a good spectacle of fisticuffs. When the gambler and the Mexican returned to the café for their evening meal, the young waitress tried to convince Ortiz that the fight was futile and that he would be hurt, if not killed, by the Irish champion.

Pablo thanked her for her concern but assured her that he was capable of beating Señor Ryan. What made him more determined was the fact that he had asked Lee Brent about the money he had been promised and the gambler had assured him that half the money they made on the fight would be his.

* * *

Two days later, on the land that was called the meadow, the people of Tucson gathered for the challenge fight. Half the proceeds from the dollar admission charge went straight into the town's coffers.

In the centre of the field was a single-roped enclosure. In one corner of the roped square stood the young Mexican, Ortiz, and Brent. In the opposite corner, stood Pat Ryan with Gallagher, the saloon-owner.

'It's like old times Patrick, mi'boy,'

Gallagher said, as his fingers kneaded and dug into the big muscled shoulders of Ryan, who stood glowering at the young Mexican in the corner opposite him. Gallagher proffered a drink of water to the Irish boxer, who gargled and spat out the liquid. 'Have all the bets been covered by the gambler?' Ryan muttered, eyeing Brent who stood with Pablo Ortiz.

'Yes, don't worry. Do what you have to do,' the saloon-owner answered. 'The man's shelled out all he had. Even his horse and saddle.'

Lee Brent looked at the big Irish fighter. Had he let the young Mexican take on too much? He was not worried about losing the money, he could always get another grubstake; it was the young waitress, Katherine, who had set doubts in his mind. She had actually begged Brent not to let Pablo fight Pat Ryan. She had even refused to bet on the Irishman, wanting nothing to do with what she called blood money.

Marshal Stewart climbed over the

rope and stood in the middle of the roped-off square. He pulled his gun and fired into the air. The noise of the crowd abated. He shouted to the crowd to stay off the rope and not push forward at any time. He told the people of Tucson that the two men would fight till one went down and stayed down.

Young Pablo Ortiz stood listening to the marshal but his eyes were firmly fixed on the Irishman. He studied Pat Ryan for any sign of weakness. The big muscled man looked confident. He must be nearly forty years, thought Ortiz. He looked like a man who had looked after himself.

'Clear the ring,' ordered the marshal, ducking under the rope

Lee Brent's hand touched Pablo's shoulder. 'Good luck son,' he said, as he stepped out of the ring.

Once the ring was clear of all but the two protagonists, the crowd went quiet with expectancy.

The town marshal fired his gun

again. 'OK, start fighting,' he shouted.

For a second, the young Mexican stood still as Ryan advanced tentatively towards him. Lee Brent had told Ortiz that all they owned had been put on him to beat the Irishman. Ryan threw his first punch and Ortiz danced away quickly to the centre of the square. Ryan advanced on him, fists up, elbows tucked in. Pablo looked for a gap in the muscled defence but could not see one.

He moved around in a circle, his eyes seeking a weakness, but Ryan moved with him, cutting down the space in the ring. Suddenly Ryan swung a right hook. Ortiz moved back. The rope caught at his back. As he moved away, the Irishman lashed out with his foot. The young Mexican stumbled as the boot tripped him. The crowd shouted encouragement to Patrick Ryan.

A left swing hit Ortiz on the side of his head, flooring him and sending stars flashing before his eyes. Instinctively he rolled on the ground. Then Ryan's boot crashed into his side. Ortiz continued to roll limiting the power from the kick. The Mexican found his feet and moved away quickly from Ryan, who followed him with lowering hands, anticipating delivering a finishing punch. Pablo's head cleared. The kick had surprised him. It was something he had not expected. This was supposed to be a fist fight. The young Mexican felt his anger rise. His keenness and awareness heightened. Ryan swung a powerful right punch. Pablo slipped under the blow, targeting a swift hook at the Irishman as he passed by. The speed and power of the blow brought the Irishman up short as the Mexican's fist sank into his gut. Then Ortiz moved in. His fists lashed out, relentlessly. Ryan was overwhelmed at the speed and power of the smaller man's attack. He had underrated the young Mexican. A fist exploded into the Irishman's face, jagging his teeth, ripping the inside of his mouth. More punches slammed into his solar plexus as he tried to protect his head. Then his vision blurred as he stumbled backwards around the square trying to get away from the bombardment of blows that smashed into him. He heard the words '*Gringo bastardo*' uttered close to his ear.

The Mexican cursed through tight lips as he rained punches down on the crouching Ryan, who was hanging on the rope to stop himself from falling. The Irishman's free arm flailed harmlessly about, then he was falling, but eager bystanders propped him up. Ryan heard a woman scream as his senses left him. Still the blows rained unmercifully on him. Marshal Stewart fired his gun as he climbed into the roped square. Pablo Ortiz felt hands grip him roughly and haul him off the unconscious Irishman. Somebody called out, 'Shoot the greaser.'

Lee Brent's reaction was immediate. He was in the ring, standing alongside Marshal Stewart, with his gun drawn and ready, his eyes searching the crowd for the troublemaker who had called out against the Mexican. Marshal Stewart fired into the air again. 'Break it up. The fight's over. The Mexican's the winner. Now, go about your business,' he ordered, backing up to stand closer to Brent and Ortiz. It was evident to the gambler that the marshal was taking no chances on somebody shooting Pablo Ortiz.

The crowd began to disperse.

The prostrate, bloody body of Ryan was being attended to by Gallagher and the café-owner. The dark-haired waitress, Katherine, stood shocked, staring at the fallen champion.

'The man's a vicious animal,' the café-owner kept muttering.

Gallagher stood back to let the town doctor tend to Pat Ryan, who still lay prone and inert. The doctor examined the staring, blank eyes of Ryan.

'I can't fix him up here. You'll have to get him back to my place. He's taken quite a battering.'

Pablo Ortiz stood between Brent and the marshal, rubbing his raw knuckles.

His hands were sore after the pounding he had given Ryan. He had heard the café-owner and the doctor's words and the young Mexican sighed and lowered his head. Slowly his anger abated.

If the Irishman had not kicked him, perhaps he would have controlled his temper but he knew that was unlikely. His temper was something that was unpredictable. In the past it had got him into trouble. When he suffered pain his temper rose and he had to hurt back. This he had done now. He turned his back on the Irish contingent.

'Come on, Pablo,' Lee Brent said. 'It's time we moved on. I'll get the money owing to us.'

The town marshal nodded in agreement. 'I'll see you're paid off, pronto, Brent. Your winnings will be quite an attraction if you stay around here too long. It would be advisable to make tracks out of here, as soon as you're ready.' He turned to the young Mexican, adding, 'You're quite a fighter, young man. Pleasure to watch.

Ain't seen fighting like that for a long time.'

Lee Brent and Pablo Ortiz made their way back to their lodgings and began to collect their belongings. As they prepared to leave their lodgings, they were met by the marshal and Katherine, the young Irish waitress. To Pablo's surprise, Ed Stewart sent the young Mexican off with Katherine, for a short walk, while he settled unfinished business with Lee Brent.

They walked in silence for a while before Katherine stopped and turned to face Pablo.

'You must not blame yourself for what happened to Pat Ryan,' she said. 'Fighters have to expect that sort of thing.' She paused and waited but Pablo said nothing. 'He's making a recovery. He's going to get better.' Pablo nodded but still remained silent. Katherine felt she did not know this man. He was not the blushing boy she had met in the café. She fidgeted with embarrassment. He seemed so much older than her now. What had happened to him?

'We'd better get back. Marshal Stewart said not to be long and I've got to get back to the café.'

The two young people joined Lee Brent and the marshal, and Katherine said her formal goodbyes. Pablo Ortiz watched her hurry away. How could he explain to her how he felt, what he had to do? It was best left unsaid. Katherine entered the café without looking back.

Pablo turned his attention to the two men.

'I've seen a few fist fights especially in the South,' the marshal was saying. 'There's money to be made on the paddle-boats on the Mississippi. The boats go out to the middle of the river, tie up and fights are put on between house slaves. There's money to be made and lost. I've seen men killed in river-boat fist fights and seen some killed for losing them. It's a game that pays, but it sure has its ugly side. Talking about ugly side, I'd better go and see how Pat Ryan and Gallagher are bearing up. I take it you two'll have left town while I'm at the saloon.'

The gambler and the Mexican fighter made their way to the livery to get their horses and settle up. Mounted, they made their way south-east, out of Tucson, over $2,000 richer than when they entered it.

The words of the marshal still echoed in Lee Brent's head and, as they rode, the two friends discussed their future. They decided to try the paddle-steamers.

'I will fight, Señor Brent, till I have enough money to buy myself a ranch with many horses. Then I will show Don Felipe I am a man of honour and not one who abuses women.'

Lee Brent listened, once more, to Ortiz repeat his aim in life. While the fire burnt so fiercely in the young Mexican's breast, his future was secure. He readily agreed to help Pablo Ortiz to achieve his goal.

5

The town of Rossville was built on the banks of the Mississippi River years before the Civil War. It took its name from the family who owned the nearby large plantation. John Ross, the present owner, had lost two sons in the Civil War. His third son, Daniel, had come through the Battle of the States unscathed and had returned to the Ross plantation to take up where he had left off, working with his father who was still active, though now in his seventies.

John Ross climbed down from his buggy, outside the livery. Turning to the Negro who held the reins he said, 'Ezra, take the buggy in and see to the horse yourself, then you and Mose follow us over to the steamer.' With his son, he ambled over to the levee where the paddle-steamer *Mississippi Queen* was moored. Captain Will Turner was leaning over the side, checking a gang of men struggling up the gang-way with the prerequisites for the coming evening's entertainment.

He eased himself up and shouted a greeting to his old acquaintance. 'Good day, Mr Ross, Daniel. Where's your boy? I hope he's OK. I've heard a lot about him.'

John Ross smiled as he looked up. 'You'll see soon enough, Turner. He's over at the livery helping Ezra,' the old man retorted. Captain Turner smiled to himself, he knew he'd get no more information out of John Ross. He had seen the buggy enter town and had studied the big-shouldered young Negro sitting alongside Ezra, the driver. He looked loose-limbed and able, and the captain had decided, there and then, to chance a few dollars on him.

Turner moved towards the gangplank, calling down to John Ross, 'There's food and drink waiting for you gentlemen. You know the way.'

86

Acknowledging the captain with a wave of their hands, Ross and his son disappeared along the ship's deck. Entering the salon, they joined a number of local businessmen who were standing about, eating and drinking. Looking around, Ross spotted Alvin Hughes, of the Rolling H ranch with his foreman, Brock, standing alongside him, a .45 pistol tied low on his hip.

The rancher came across to greet him, his hand outstretched. 'John,' he said. The two old adversaries shook hands.

'Where's your boy?' Hughes asked, looking about. 'You haven't got cold feet, have you?'

'You should know the Ross family don't have cold feet — not unless they're dead,' old man Ross retorted.

It was then that the two Negroes entered the salon. Ezra's was a familiar face, but the paler youth was new to the rancher. Hughes looked him over.

'Is that your new fighter, John? Is he any good?'

John Ross smiled. 'You'll know when he gets into the ring with your man.'

Hughes smirked, 'He's light-coloured, John. Is he one of your own?'

Daniel Ross made to move threateningly towards Hughes, but his father stopped him.

'No, son, let it go. Mr Hughes is using jibes to rile us.' Turning to the rancher, he continued, 'He could be one of mine, Alvin. Don't you wish you could make one like him yourself?'

'I'm quite satisfied with things as they are and if you're so sure of your man, how about increasing our side bet to twenty thousand dollars?' Hughes countered.

'Done,' came the quick reply. Old man Ross smiled to himself as they shook hands on it. Hughes had taken the bait.

The plantation owner had become aware of the young fighter when one of his overseers had come upon the young Negro fighting over one of the

88

women workers on his plantation. He had reported it to John Ross who had done what he always did and organized a fight between the two men involved with all the workers watching. Whoever won claimed whatever the dispute had been about. The young man had greatly impressed John Ross with his fistic ability and he had been put to work with Ezra, an experienced fist-fighter, who had fought for John Ross before. John Ross expected great things from the young fighter.

'Is the food up to its usual standards?' Ross asked, changing the subject. Hughes nodded. Captain Turner could be relied upon to supply a fair table with the ten-dollar entry fee he charged each person who boarded.

John Ross joined the crowd mulling around the laden tables. He was inundated with questions about his fighter, who by now had retired with Ezra to one of the cabins to get ready.

His man was the main topic of

conversation, being new to the game, whilst Hughes's fighter was well known and unbeaten.

'All I'll say is my boy will beat the Dutchman. I'm not saying any more than that. I'm betting to win,' John Ross concluded, and moved away to speak to others in the gathering. The businessmen were soon joined by a bevy of beauties whose arrival was announced in glowing terms by the captain, who had shipped the women aboard for the men's enjoyment at a price to be discreetly settled after the fight. The scene became livelier and the betting increased with the flow of liquor.

Both the fighters were now in the salon, stripped to the waist, on view for the punters and, hopefully, to encourage further betting. The difference between the two men was their age, their build and their origin. Larson, the Dutchman, was a thirty-year-old, thickset giant of a man, with a mane of yellow hair, who glanced around him with confidence, before approaching the rancher, who was his boss and sponsor. Ross's coffee-coloured fighter was much younger, leaner-waisted and well muscled. His physique and lithe youthfulness impressed the men gathered there. Ezra escorted the young fighter over to where John Ross and his son were standing.

Captain Turner rubbed his hands together as he made his way back to the head of the gangway. He reckoned his percentage of the betting should be a very satisfactory one.

Alvin Hughes was also very pleased at the way things were going. A lot of money was being placed on the unknown Negro and the rancher was covering many of the side bets. Hughes knew his man, Larson, was a good, experienced fighter, who had time and again proved his worth. He had made short work of every opponent he had met so far, including John Ross's Negro, Ezra.

'That plantation owner's got more

money than sense,' he smirked to his foreman, as he noticed John Ross talking to his two Negroes. He saw Ross call over one of the women who laughed and nodded agreement to whatever he was saying.

Ross was telling Mose, his fighter, that she would be there for his enjoyment if he beat Alvin Hughes's fighter. The young fighter was wide-eyed at what his employer was saying. He had never pleasured a white woman. Now his employer had promised him one. The white woman was pretty and young. Mose licked his lips. He would win the fight. He could feel his excitement as he thought of his reward.

'Remember this, Mose. You win, she's yours. We won't even consider the alternative.' John Ross's cold stare looked deep into the young fighter's face. He saw smouldering desire and hunger. There was no trace of fear.

Daniel Ross moved off with his father, 'Don't you think you went a bit far offering a white woman to the black, even if she is white trash, Pa?'

John Ross smirked at his son's question, adding, 'There'll be no woman here for him, son. Just a carrot on a stick . . . a very long stick,' he grinned, 'He'll be able to have his pick of any girl at the plantation, with or without my say-so when this is over. If necessary I'd have offered him six white women to get that gleam in his eye and put the fire in his loins. You saw his reaction. He'll beat the Dutchman for me and win me twenty thousand dollars.'

On the levee, Lee Brent studied the *Mississippi Queen*. The men with money strolled up the gangplank. He took note of the captain who stood on deck, greeting each individual as they stepped aboard.

'It's about time we joined them,' the gambler said to Ortiz.

They had left their horses at the town livery stables. The owner had answered Brent's questions about the large number of animals being accommodated. Some had been tethered two and three abreast to a stall.

'There's to be a fight aboard the old steam-paddler,' he had told them. 'It sails in two hours.'

Lee Brent studied his time piece, it read three o'clock.

'Can you tell me more?' the gambler asked, tossing the ostler an extra dollar.

'John Ross has brought in one of his Blacks to fight Alvin Hughes's man. It should be some fight for as long as it lasts. Hughes's man is undefeated. He's a Dutchman. They say he's getting too old, but then they've been saying that for some time. If you have ten dollars to spare it will get you aboard the *Mississippi Queen*, then you'll need extra money if you want to wager.'

The ostler went off to see to other riders entering his livery. He rubbed his hands. Money was pouring in today. 'They should have these fights every day,' he muttered to himself.

Lee Brent and the young Mexican went to find a boarding-house, have a meal and freshen up before making their way to the paddle-steamer. Captain Turner stood watching the pair as they started up the gangplank.

'No greasers allowed on board,' he shouted. The gambler stopped.

'Where does it say that?'

'I say it and it's my boat,' the captain answered. 'Now, get out of the way or get aboard but without the Mex.'

Lee Brent turned to go but he suddenly had an idea. 'I take it John Ross is aboard?'

The captain was taken by surprise at the question.

'You take it right . . . and his fighter. Who wants to know?'

'Lee Brent, and this Mexican is here to challenge the winner of today's fight.'

Captain Turner studied Ortiz. He did not look like a fighter. It might be right what the man said, but John Ross had not mentioned it nor had Alvin Hughes.

'Pay your ten dollars but keep your

Mex out of sight. He's not to mix with the rest of the company. I'll be down to check as soon as I get under way and if I find out you're lying to me you'll both go overboard.'

'I'll stay here, Señor Brent, you go on ahead,' Pablo offered, but the gambler shook his head.

'If it's OK with the captain, it's OK with me, and I want you to see what the fighters are like.'

The young Mexican hesitantly climbed the boarding plank. Brent paid the twenty dollars and, taking Ortiz by the elbow, ushered him across the boards. The gambler studied the crowd that milled about on the deck of the paddle-steamer. They were sampling the food and drink that was still available as they chatted between themselves and although there were a number of stares in their direction, nobody openly questioned the appearance of Pablo Ortiz.

A sudden surge shuddered the boat as the wheels began to turn and the

Mississippi Queen slowly pulled away from the levee. The crowd on deck watched the shoreline for a while before making their way to the comfort of the salon to take their places for the forthcoming entertainment. Lee Brent and Pablo Ortiz stood at the rear of the seated crowd.

The paddle-steamer shuddered to a stop in the middle of the river and the boat settled gracefully at anchor. The captain entered the salon to take his place at the ringside and duly declared, 'Gentlemen, and ladies, the time has come for the highlight of the evening. If all are ready, let the proceedings begin.' Laughter and cheers greeted his announcement, but the banter died down as the two protagonists entered the ring.

Lee Brent watched the two Negroes as they walked towards the ring. The younger one was well built and catlike in his stride. His body was covered with a layer of muscle, rippling and loose. The other Negro was older and walked with a slight limp. They climbed into the ring.

Lee Brent glanced at his young companion. Ortiz was studying the young Negro's every move as he punched out, shadow-boxing to the instructions of his corner man. It was evident to both the gambler and the young Mexican that this was organized fighting. Brent's attention was drawn to an old man who stood up from his chair, went to the Negro's corner, said something to the younger man, then resumed his seat.

'That could possibly be John Ross,' Brent mused to himself.

The crowd's attention was now drawn to the other side of the ring as Alvin Hughes approached and walked towards the roped square. Behind him lumbered the huge Dutchman — his hair flaxen; his neck seemingly non-existent; his head looked to be stuck on to his shoulders. It was Alvin Hughes who stood in the corner as Larson climbed into the ring. The big

Dutchman acknowledged the crowd before casting his gaze over to the young Negro's corner. He was at least sixty pounds heavier than him.

Ezra, the older Negro, began to work on Mose, rubbing the back of his neck and shoulders, while giving him last-minute advice. The young black fighter nodded, eyes narrowed and deep in concentration.

The instruction and warm-up proceedings were all new to both Lee Brent and Pablo Ortiz. The gambler realized instantly that he would need to get someone to advise and train his young Mexican friend. Up to now Pablo Ortiz had done well, but if he was to fight in organized matches, advice was needed.

Most bets had been laid and covered but some of the bets had been delayed. Now on seeing the bulk of Hughes's man, the punters' minds had been made up for them.

A very officious Captain Turner, minus his cap, climbed into the ring.

'Gentlemen, the warm-up time is over. You've had your last chance to place your bets. All that is left to do is to remind the fighters of the rules.' With that he signalled both men to the centre of the ring. He told them, in a loud voice that could be heard all round the ship's deck, that if either of them could not toe the line in the centre of the ring, after being knocked down and after receiving attention for a minute from his corner man, the fight was to end. The man left on his feet was to be proclaimed the winner.

'If you've got that, get back to your corner and come out fighting when I give the signal.'

The Dutchman and the Negro were primed and ready. At the signal they both moved forward and began circling each other.

The crowd settled back to watch the two contestants. The atmosphere was tense and electric. The gambler wondered where the heavy betting lay, was it with power and experience or with youth and energy? The young Mexican studied both fighters from a different angle. The lumbering bulk of the fighting Dutchman and the loose-limbed agility of the tall Negro.

The Dutchman looked immovable; his massive form seemed to fill the ring as he crouched and circled, waiting for the Negro to make a move forward. Ortiz immediately saw that the roped ring was not big enough for Mose to use evading tactics, which he himself would have used if ever he fought Larson.

The ringsiders began to get restless and cries to move in and fight were shouted to the black man who stood balanced on his toes, circling the ring. The Dutchman shuffled forward. Mose's left fist shot out as Larson closed in, the punch solid in its delivery. The hulk before him did not even seem aware of the blow. He angled and moved forward again as the young Black backed off and circled him. Larson inched ever closer.

Mose's left fist shot out again. Larson leaned into it, taking the blow and grabbing out at the fist. Catching Mose by the wrist, he moved crab-like, pulling the young Black towards him onto a mighty swinging punch. The young Negro's legs buckled. The Dutchman clubbed him again, holding Mose fast to the spot. As the Negro began to fall to his knees, Larson let go of his wrist and powered a mighty blow across the side of his head, sending him crashing to the floor. Mose's head jolted back and he lay stunned at the Dutchman's feet. Larson peered down at his opponent before ambling back to his corner.

Hughes patted the Dutchman on the shoulder. Ezra jumped into the ring and helped his injured protégé to his corner. A bucket of ice water was hastily provided and Ezra tried desperately to revive the semi-conscious fighter. The water ran down Mose's face and chest. His eyes flickered and began to focus. The Dutchman walked to the centre of the ring. All eyes turned to Mose as he struggled to consciousness. Still groggy and heavy on his heels he was pushed forward to meet his antagonist. Larson smashed a powerful right punch into the face of the young Negro. The blow could be heard around the ringside as it crashed home. The jaw of the young Black was smashed and broken. His body landed in his corner.

Ezra knelt beside Mose and then looked anxiously over to John Ross who was now on his feet, leaning forward to study his young fighter.

The Dutchman stood in the centre of the ring waiting. The silence of the spectators lay heavy in the air. John Ross's eyes left the ring to stare at Hughes who was standing outside the roped square. Alvin Hughes smirked at his old adversary. It was not the first time that the plantation owner had brought in one of his black workers to fight his Dutchman. First, it had been Ezra; now, it was his protégé.

Hughes had found the Dutchman in New York where he had seen him in action in a bar brawl. He had liked what he had seen and had hired him for the sole purpose of beating John Ross at the game Ross had started years ago with great success when the plantation owners encouraged the slaves to fight for their masters. A lot of money had always been wagered. Hughes had brought the Dutchman back to his ranch after the Civil War when fist-fighting had been renewed once the plantations were resettled and prosperity returned to the area. John Ross and his associates had taken to staging the fist fights on board the paddle-steamers moored in the centre of the river to escape interference from the law or any other unwanted persons. Betting on the outcome of the fist fights became a money-making business once again. Fortunes were lost and won and tonight he, Alvin Hughes, was $20,000 better off.

The minute allowed for in the rules

passed and Captain Turner called for Mose to toe the centre line. The young Negro lay unconscious in his corner, his face smashed by the mighty onslaught of the Dutchman, who was proving to be invincible. His last two fights had been against John Ross's Negroes, first Ezra and today Mose. Previously, Larson had crippled Ezra by stamping on his knee after he had downed him. The injury had left Ezra with a permanent limp and had dashed John Ross's hopes of beating his adversary. The injured Negro had trained Mose to take his place, but sadly it had been to no avail.

John Ross listened while the town doctor examined and diagnosed the extent of Mose's injury; he had a broken jaw. The plantation owner sighed, that was another one of his pugilists who had cost him a high price in a lost wager to Hughes.

The engines of the paddle-steamer once again shook the vessel into movement and slowly the *Mississippi*

Queen eased its way back to the riverside. Those who wished to would disembark, including John Ross's fighter who was to be taken back to the plantation with Ezra. Then the big boat would cruise back down the river while the clients and guests of Captain Turner continued to enjoy the amenities for the remainder of the evening and possibly late into the night.

Lee Brent had watched the fight without comment. He had not been overly surprised at the outcome. Power and experience stood a good chance against youth and energy. He was, however, glad he had decided against a wager. He looked at Pablo Ortiz to see his reaction, but the young Mexican did not seem perturbed or surprised at the result.

As the engines throbbed into action the crowd began to mill about again. There were a number of people now forming card schools at a few of the tables whilst others were going off to cabins to sample the favours of the working girls.

Lee Brent was keen to get into a card game, but he wondered if the remaining passengers would continue to accept the presence of Pablo Ortiz. The Mexican seemed to read his mind.

'When the boat stops, I will go back to the lodging-house while you stay and see if the Dutchman will fight me. I will see you later.'

Brent was surprised at Pablo's request. 'Surely you don't want to fight him after seeing what he did to that young Negro?'

'*Si*, I will fight him if you are willing to gamble our money?' the Mexican said.

Brent noticed John Ross and his son standing in conversation with the captain, outside the salon door.

'Come with me, Pablo, I have an idea?' he said, and the two made their way out on to the deck.

'Excuse me, Mr Ross.' Lee Brent said, addressing the old man. The plantation owner looked up.

'Yes?'

'My name's Lee Brent. I'm a gambler by profession.'

Recognizing the gambler and the Mexican, Captain Turner said, 'Do you know these men, John?'

'No,' said the plantation owner.

The ship's captain called over two of his crew. 'Throw these two overboard. I warned them of the consequences when they boarded. He looks like a conman and I won't have his type or greasers on board my ship.'

One of the crew reached out for Pablo Ortiz who stepped back, knocking the crewman's hand down.

'I won't go. I can't swim.' There was panic in the Mexican's voice.

Both crewmen then centred their attention on the young Mexican. As they grabbed for him he shot fast sharp punches to both their heads and they staggered back away from the fighting madman. Lee Brent had pulled his gun and the space around them cleared as silence fell on the group.

'I don't want any trouble. I just want to speak to Mr Ross,' he told the captain.

The plantation owner stood waiting for Brent to say more. The gambler introduced Pablo Ortiz and told John Ross about his fighting abilities. The old man smiled. 'I've just had a quick demonstration.'

At this point, the captain interrupted, 'He said he knew you and that he had brought this greaser on board at your request to fight the winner.'

Ross studied the Mexican. He was not as tall as he would have liked but there was something about Ortiz — the strong jawline, powerful neck and shoulders, his stance solid and well balanced.

'What else do you do for a living, besides fighting that is?' he asked Pablo.

'I am a *remudero, señor* — a good one.'

'A horse wrangler,' mused John Ross;

that accounted for his powerful frame. Wrangling was a job that required strength in legs and arms but that alone did not make a good fighter.

'Do you think you could beat the Dutchman?'

Ross did not see any doubt in the expression of Pablo Ortiz as he answered. 'Yes.'

John Ross turned to his son. 'We'll go ashore now, Daniel, we are going home.'

The scuffle between the two crew members and Ortiz had not caused too much of a stir. It was quickly forgotten as the plantation owner Ross reassured the captain and the crew members saying that there had been a misunderstanding. Then Ross went to find Hughes who was celebrating his victory with some of his cronies.

'Congratulations, Alvin, I'll be in touch,' he told the rancher.

'Aren't you staying over, John, or have you had enough excitement for one day?' Hughes taunted.

John Ross let the sarcasm go over his head. 'Something important has turned up,' he replied.

Nodding to the rest of the company, he left the salon and joined his son, Daniel, with Ezra and Mose, Pablo and Lee Brent at the rail while the paddle-steamer lazed up to the river bank.

Leaving the boat, John Ross stopped on the levee long enough to invite the gambler and the Mexican to visit him at the Ross plantation.

'Think it over,' the old man said as he climbed into the buggy.

'What do you think. Pablo?' Lee Brent asked, as they made their way back to their lodgings.

'I think we can make some money, *señor*, if you are willing to trust me.'

'That Dutchman's one powerful being,' the gambler reminded his friend.

The young Mexican stopped and grabbed Brent's arm. 'In that ring he is like a bear in a cage. Maybe there is no bear without the cage.'

111

'Maybe, young Pablo, maybe.' The gambler's thoughts returned once again to the profit they could make. The problem was he really would prefer to bet on a sure thing.

6

The journey to the Ross plantation did not take too long. As they traversed the seemingly endless stretch of cotton fields, the two travellers were surprised at the size of the domain. Further along the road, geometric plots of vegetables, fruit trees and bushes led them to the first sign of habitation. Neat rows of the Negro-workers' one-storey houses edged the road, behind their picket fences. The whole plantation looked impressive and prosperous. In the near distance, they could make out the main ranch and outbuildings and Brent and Ortiz increased their horses' gait as they neared their objective. The smell of horses and stables hung in the air as the outbuildings came into view alongside of the main house. It was a huge place, two storeys high with a wooden balcony that served the house.

As they came alongside the stables, Ezra was there to meet them.

'Mr Ross is expecting you. If you will wait a minute I'll stable your horses and take you over to the big house.'

John Ross, who was sitting on the veranda with his son and daughter-in-law, stood up to welcome his visitors. 'You've met my son, Daniel, and this is his wife, Helen.'

Lee Brent, faintly surprised to see the woman dressed in denim trousers and a shirt, doffed his hat and shook hands. Helen Ross's cool gaze swept over the gambler and behind him to the young Mexican.

'And this is the young hothead who took on Captain Turner's crew last night. He reckons he's a top-notch *remudero*. I'll leave you to judge his efficiency, while I have a talk with his *patron*, Mr Brent.'

'*Señora, señors.*' Pablo Ortiz acknowledged the introduction with lowered head.

'Then we will go and see what the

114

young man has to offer,' Helen said, stepping down from the veranda. 'And your name is?'

'Ortiz, Pablo Ortiz, *señora*,' the young Mexican said, stumbling a pace behind her as she set off to the corrals behind the stables.

John Ross called for Maisie, the black house-keeper, to bring coffee, and the three men sat down to chat.

'I won't waste your time, Mr Ross. I'll come straight to the point. Young Ortiz has potential to be a great fist-fighter, but he lacks training and guidance. I have been willing to fund his activities, but I have no expert knowledge of the rules of the organized fight game. If you are willing, we are prepared to work for you if, in return, you will consider training Ortiz. If you are not satisfied with either our work or his progress we'll move on.'

'Well, you certainly have it all planned out, Brent. I must say I like a man to know his mind and to speak it but it's your young protégé

I'm interested in. I've no intention of feeding you two for free, so what exactly do you have to offer?'

At that moment the housekeeper arrived with the coffee.

Lee Brent watched as she poured the steaming cups before answering.

'I'm a gambler by profession, which is of little use on a plantation. I'm keen to keep close to young Ortiz while he's in training. I figure I could be some help in that area. I'm not looking for free board. I reckon I can pay my way, for the time being.'

The old man smiled. 'I wasn't thinking of starting a hotel on the plantation but I take your point. I am interested in your Mexican. My man Ezra knows the fist game. He used to be my best fighter till Larson crippled his knee. He can work out with the Mex and judge his worth. Till then you are welcome to stay as a guest in my home.'

Pablo Ortiz accompanied Helen Ross to one of the corrals containing four

116

young horses. Ezra was saddling up the largest of them, ready to be ridden. Ortiz grinned as he looked over the excellent specimens of horseflesh.

'These are fine animals, *señora*. You are very lucky. I would be privileged to work with them.'

'They look good but they can be mean if they get the chance,' Helen Ross retorted.

Ezra led the saddled horse out of the corral.

'The King is ready to ride Miss Helen.' The Negro passed over the reins as he glanced enquiringly at the young Mexican.

'This is Ezra,' she said, swinging herself agilely into the saddle. 'While I'm off on my ride, he can show you the stables. You'll work and sleep there if Daddy Ross agrees to let you stay.'

Helen Ross gathered the reins and gently tugged to one side. Ortiz noted that the horse responded well.

'Check him out with the horses, Ezra. He says he's a *remudero*. He'll be working with you if he's any good.'

With that she tapped the horse's flank with her heels and loped away. Pablo watched the horse and rider gradually pick up speed as they rapidly disappeared from view.

'The *señora* rides well,' he said, admiringly.

'Miss Helen knows her horses as well as any top wrangler. You'd better be good or she'll not let you near them,' Ezra said, moving away from the rail. They made their way to the stable block that housed many of the animals. It was a two-storey building with living quarters for the stablehands above the stalls. Ezra noticed the young Mexican's enquiring look as he limped into the stables. 'I broke my leg fighting. I was kicked and stomped by the big Dutchman, the same one who broke Mose's face last night.'

'That is why I am here, Señor Ezra. I intend to finish that Dutchman. I am Pablo Ortiz. I am a fighter.'

Ezra stopped and looked the young

man over. 'Just call me Ezra and I'll call you Pablo. I heard about your brawl with the boatmen but fighting in a ring is different.' he said.

'*Si*, I know this. I see this last night. I need your help, Ezra, to do it properly. Believe me, I can fight . . . I have fought before . . . I *need* to fight.'

'You mean fist-fighting is your idea? It's not the idea of the gambler?'

'No. It is my decision. I fight; I get money; I return to Mexico; I get back my good name,' Ortiz stated with vehemence.

Ezra began to look at the young Mexican through new eyes. Here was a man who was not being forced or coerced into fighting. The fighters he had known so far had either been fighting at their owner's behest or had been talked into it with empty promises of riches by unscrupulous manipulators who sought to make a fast buck.

'Your gambler friend? He's not just using you?' he asked.

'Using me? Nobody uses Pablo Ortiz.

Señor Lee Brent is my friend. He takes care of me and I fight both for him and myself.'

'What kind of friend wants you to fight the Dutchman?' Ezra countered.

Ortiz laughed. 'It was I who said that I would fight the Dutchman, not Señor Brent.'

'Well, good luck then. Perhaps you will have more luck than me and Mose.'

With that, Ezra limped across the floor towards the stairs that led to the upper floor. A young Negro boy came out of the tackle room, at the back of the stables, and punched at a bag of some sort, which was hanging heavily from the wooden rafters. The bag barely moved.

'Can you teach me to hit harder, Mr Ezra?' the boy asked. Pablo was aware of the respect in the youngster's voice.

'When you get bigger. Now get busy with that broom and clean out this place. Where's that rascal Jude? He's supposed to be helping you.'

'He's taken the visitor's saddle-bags over to the big house. Mister Ross sent for them,' the young Negro explained. 'And I've put his bag upstairs, like I was told,' he concluded, pointing towards Ortiz.

Ezra nodded and began to climb the stairs. Ortiz followed, conscious of the stable boy watching his every movement as he resumed his chores. At the top of the stairs, Ezra paused as he opened the door. 'In here,' he said. Ortiz followed him into a large room containing two cots, a cupboard and a chest of drawers at one end and a table and two chairs at the other. A clean, rag rug covered the wooden floor.

'This is my room. If you stay, you will share it with me. Keep yourself clean and tidy and there'll be no problem.'

The young Mexican went over to his bag, which had been placed on one of the beds 'If it is OK with you that I stay, I will give you no problems,'

Ortiz assured Ezra, opening his bag and lifting out a roll of dirty washing. The few clean clothes he had he took out more carefully and looked towards the big Negro.

'There's empty drawers over there for you to use,' Ezra said, indicating the chest.

That done, the young Mexican searched in his bag again. This time he took out his .45 and placed it in the drawer with his clothes. Ezra's eyes widened at the sight of the gun.

'The boss don't allow his workers having guns, no sir. If Mr Ross sees that, you'll be thrown out mighty quick.' The big Negro shook his head as he continued, 'Only Mr Daniel carries a gun and he sure knows how to use it.'

'It is no problem, Ezra, do not worry. I have no use for it here. See, I have put it away till I leave this place.' Ortiz closed the drawer. Picking up his small bundle of dirty washing, he made for the door.

'Where are you going with that?' Ezra asked.

'I need to wash these. I have not a lot of spare clothes.'

Ezra took the soiled clothing from him. 'I know a nice girl who will wash them for you.'

'No one will slave for me,' Ortiz said firmly, 'I can see to my own clothes.'

'Slave? Who's talking 'bout slave?' Ezra gasped before bursting out laughing. 'You sure have got the wrong end of the stick my young Mexican friend. Slavery is over. We Negroes who work the plantation stay here because we want to. Those who chose different, left. But those who had any sense stayed. Mister Ross is a fair boss — strict but fair, always was . . . Now come on.'

Pablo Ortiz followed the big Negro to one of the buildings where steam was oozing out of the doorway and window apertures.

'Take care of these, Mabel. Good care of them. They belong to my young friend here,' Ezra called as they entered the steamy interior. A middle-aged woman popped out from behind a steaming boiler. She took the clothing, looking quizzically at the few threadbare pieces.

'They won't stand much of a wash,' she chuckled throatily, as she tossed the clothes into a bowl. Ezra kissed her cheek as he patted her ample rump.

'Get out of here, you big horny toad,' she said, swinging a piece of wet washing at him. Ezra dodged away, automatically. His face twisted in pain as his leg buckled under him but he managed to keep upright as he staggered out of the range of the sodden cloth. He laughed, with some effort, as he limped heavily out of the laundry.

'You'll get them later, washed and pressed,' he told Ortiz, adding with a chuckle, 'You'll have to pay . . . no slave works here.'

They made their way past the stables to the corralled horses. Ortiz saw how good the stock of blood mares and their colts were. He studied the fine lines of each animal.

'These horses look too good to be pulling carts and buggies,' Ortiz commented.

'They belong to Miss Helen. She rides them and only the best will do. She will be entering King Cotton, the horse you saw her on before, in the Kentucky Stakes, next month.'

Pablo Ortiz's eyes lit up. 'I used to ride in races in Mexico. It would be good to get back on such a horse as this.'

'We best see how well you perform, my riding, fighting, Mexican friend. You can help me with the horses and then, when we're done, I will put you through a work-out with me in the stable,' said Ezra.

Pablo eagerly agreed, only too willing to show his skill with horses. With regards to the work-out it would be interesting to see what the Negro had in store.

While the Negro and the young

Mexican went about their chores, Lee Brent was being shown over the plantation by Daniel, the son of the owner. The gambler could see that the workers, mostly black, looked healthy and seemed well contented as they toiled in the fields. Daniel Ross told him that most of the Negroes were children of past slaves who had chosen to stay at the Ross plantation after they had been freed. It spoke well of the Ross family that not many of their slaves, when offered the choice, left to go north-east to the big cities, looking for riches that were not there.

The two men later returned to the house where John Ross sat waiting on the veranda. After refreshments the three men made their way to the stables. They arrived at the same time as Ezra and the young Mexican.

'He works well, Mr Ross. I can use him if you decide he can stay,' Ezra said.

'That will depend on him,' John

Ross replied. 'You know what to do.'
Ezra nodded.

It was evident to Lee Brent that
what was going to happen had been
prearranged by the old plantation
owner. Ezra called for the younger
Negro boys to bring seats and Jude
and his friend brought three chairs for
John Ross, his son and Brent to sit on.
The youngsters retired to a nearby stall.
They knew that if they kept quiet, they
would be allowed to stay and watch.

'Have you informed our young friend
what's expected of him?' John Ross
asked Ezra.

'Not yet, Mr Ross,' the Negro
answered.

'Well get on with it,' he was ordered.

The big Negro took Pablo to one
side. 'Take off your shirt and boots
and put these on,' he said, conjuring
up a pair of moccasins. Ortiz looked
puzzled.

'Mister Ross wants to see you work
out,' Ezra said, stripping off his own
shirt and revealing a well-muscled body

with arms and shoulders to match. The young Mexican did likewise, displaying a no less impressive build.

'Tell him what you want him to do,' John Ross said.

'You fight with me and see if you can land a punch. I will defend myself and try to hit you.'

Standing opposite Ezra, who had stepped back a few paces, Pablo Ortiz gathered his thoughts. It was obviously time to let the plantation owner and Ezra see how adept he was as a fighter.

'Show him how good you are, Pablo. That's what we are here for,' Brent confirmed.

The young Mexican took a few deep breaths, nodded to Ezra and began to circle with raised fists. The big Negro, his crippled leg behind him, moved cagily. It was evident to Pablo that Ezra would find it difficult to move around with agility. The Mexican tried a left swing. The Negro slipped the punch, moving his body from the waist, and replied with a left hook. Ortiz slipped under it to find a right uppercut landing on his nose. He staggered back surprised at the Negro's hand speed and the ferocity of the punch. Thankfully, Ezra's leg injury handicapped him and he could not follow up his advantage. Ortiz's nose stung and his eyes had begun to water.

'This is a work-out, my friend?' he muttered to himself, wiping the blood dripping from his nose. He felt his anger rise and his survival instinct came into play. He began to move around Ezra. The Negro turned to follow him. Suddenly, Ortiz moved forward, both fists lashing out. The punches reined into the big Negro who had difficulty getting out of the way.

Ezra had been told by John Ross to take as much advantage as he could of the inexperienced young Mexican. John Ross valued Ezra as a fighter, even one with a bad leg. The big Negro had fought many times for the plantation owner over the years, starting during the time when Negroes had been forced to fight for their owners. Even at his advanced age, he had been undefeated till his encounter with Larson. Since then, the plantation owner had been impressed by the Negro's training of young Mose but he had not been the right man for the job — the job of fixing the Dutchman once and for all. John Ross was searching for the right man.

The old man had been unimpressed with the start of the work-out but now things were livening up. The bloody-nosed young Mex seemed to have the ability to throw punches from every direction. His power and speed was awesome. Ezra was brought up short by a right-hand punch to the head. Then his body doubled over as a left swing buried itself into his stomach. He staggered back, his bad leg hindering his movements. The Mexican followed, lashing out, his lips moving silently as he cursed the man before him.

Lee Brent decided it was time to stop and got to his feet. John Ross's hand caught hold of his leg, 'Sit down,' he hissed, his eyes sparkling as he watched Ezra retreating, only his fighting instincts keeping him on his feet. Blows exploded on Ezra's chin with tremendous speed and power and finally the legs of the big Negro buckled. Ezra crumpled to the floor in a heap. The young Mexican stood gasping for air at the exertion of his frenzied onslaught. The stable was silent except for a strangled cry from one of the stalls.

'You two, get out here,' the old man shouted. The two stableboys obeyed his command, with guilty, 'Yes sir, Mr Ross sir.'

'Get a bucket of water and some cloths and see to Ezra,' John Ross said, turning away from the big Negro's still form, to study the young Mexican's compact physique — the muscled whipcord arms and chest that rose and fell as Pablo recovered from his exertion — with the same interest he would show in purchasing a new horse.

Lee Brent dropped his head to his chest and smiled to himself. He had seen Ortiz fight before but even he was surprised at what he had just witnessed.

'I take it you are interested in our proposal, Mr Ross,' the gambler said.

The old man turned from Ortiz to address Lee Brent.

'Come to the house. I want to talk to you and the young Mex.'

Grabbing his shirt, Ortiz joined the gambler and they followed the plantation owner and his son, leaving the stableboys to tend to Ezra. Old John Ross seemed to have found an added zip to his walk as he climbed the few steps to the house veranda. He called Maisie to bring refreshments, then he sat on the chair by the table.

'Sit down,' he said, indicating the chairs. The gambler joined the Ross men but Pablo preferred to lean against the rail of the veranda, taking in long breaths of clean, fresh air.

'I did not believe it when you told me you had a fighter,' John Ross said, turning his head to address Ortiz. 'But you surprised me, young man. I told Ezra to work you out hard, so there won't be any resentment in that area. He's been a good fighter and he knows the fight game. He can give it out and he can take it. Ezra is handicapped because of the fight game but he will be looked after for as long as he lives.'

'Now then.' He turned his attention to Lee Brent. 'You can stay on as a guest for as long as you like. The young Mex will work for me as a *remudero*, as he wishes to call himself, during his stay here. Ezra will train him and he will fight under my name for the Ross plantation. If he beats the Dutchman I will reward him well.'

'It's up to my fighting partner,' Lee Brent replied. 'Pablo, you heard Mr Ross's proposal. The decision is yours.'

Maisie arrived with sandwiches and coffee and cut short the discussion.

Pablo Ortiz turned his back on the seated men and leant on the rail. The offer of a reward, in addition to what he and Señor Brent would make on their gamble, echoed in his ears. He knew what he wanted for a reward. He had seen the magnificent blood stock in the corrals. The acquisition of any one of those horses would be another step towards fulfilling his dreams.

'Well, Ortiz, what's your decision? Ezra will look after you and get you prepared for the fight with Larson, but you'll have to water down your punches when you're practising, if you want to have a trainer.' John Ross laughed, addressing the young Mexican, who had turned to face the three men. The old man had spoken to him with respect in his voice and it was dawning on the Mexican that he was a young man of exceptional ability. John Ross was willing to back him and possibly pay a high price, if he won. His future looked good. He was a happy young man. He would soon be able to go to Don Felipe Lopez and proclaim his innocence.

7

The refreshments and talking over, the two men left the big house and made their way to the stables. Pablo Ortiz walked in silence, his brain busily engaged in planning his future.

'Well, you heard what John Ross said. He wants you to work and fight for him. What do you think?' asked Lee Brent.

'I think, yes,' replied Ortiz, thoughtfully. 'I will stay here and train and fight this Señor Dutchman but not on a boat . . . on land.'

'Not on the steamboat . . . ' the gambler began.

'There is one more thing, Señor Brent, Señor Ross says he would reward me well . . . ' The young Mexican paused to eye his companion before blurting out, 'I would want two of his horses.'

The gambler showed his surprise, 'I thought it was the money you were after,' he said.

'I will make money when I fight the Señor Dutchman. You have said you will place money for me.'

'So I will,' the gambler confirmed, patting the money-belt around his waist, whilst shaking his head in puzzlement. Brent was pleased to find Ortiz so confident about fighting the Dutchman, but he also knew it was up to John Ross and the organizers to pick a venue. Alvin Hughes would need to agree and there was also the steamboat's captain to consider. He provided other entertainment besides the fight spectacle. The feasting, gambling and use of the imported whores provided lucrative rewards for Captain Turner.

'I'll have a word with John Ross about the venue,' Brent said.

The young Mexican smiled as he watched his friend walk off. If his plan was successful, he would be able to return to the country of his birth with money and two fine horses. He would be able to do many things. Turning on his heels he entered the stables to find Ezra still a little shaken by his earlier ordeal.

'I am here, Señor Ezra, what do you wish me to do?' he asked cheerfully.

'You can give me a hand with the corral horses,' Ezra said over his shoulder as he limped towards the far doors. Pablo hurried forward to help open them.

'Make sure you lock them back,' Ezra warned, as he put his shoulder against one of the heavy doors.

It was at that moment that Helen Ross rode into the corral adjacent to the stable.

Ezra turned his head to instruct Pablo further and stumbled, falling away from the door which slammed closed as the horse and rider passed. King Cotton reared up in surprise, catching his rider off guard. Helen Ross screamed as her feet left the stirrups and she tumbled from the animal to land heavily on her

138

left shoulder. Pablo Ortiz ran forward to restrain the frightened horse while Ezra scrambled to his feet and hastened to secure the door. Lee Brent, hearing the commotion, ran from the direction of the house to the corral. As he vaulted over the fence he saw Ortiz grappling with the animal as it reared up again, its front legs missing the prostrate woman by inches as it crashed down. Grabbing the reins, the Mexican's powerful arms pulled the beast away from Helen Ross as she struggled to rise with assistance of Lee Brent and Ezra. Ortiz held the stallion as it fought to escape, speaking soothingly but firmly till it quietened down.

Helen Ross moaned and held her shoulder as she was helped to the safety of the surrounding fence. Ezra sent one of the stableboys to tell Daniel Ross and the other to find old Maya, the healing woman.

Pablo Ortiz stood a way off with King Cotton. He stroked the quivering neck of the stallion and his softly spoken voice continued to calm the magnificent beast.

Daniel Ross came running to see what had happened, with Maisie twittering on behind him.

'Oh, Missie Helen, what has that bad horse done to you?' she wailed.

'He's not a bad horse, Maisie, and I'll be OK. We both got a fright. That's all. Now stop fussing . . . ' Helen Ross's voice tailed off as she collapsed against her husband.

'I'm sorry, Mr Daniel. I slipped and the door banged closed. I've sent the boy for old Maya . . . ' Ezra began.

'Send her over to the house,' Daniel Ross interrupted, sweeping his wife into his arms.

Lee Brent walked with him back to the house where John Ross was waiting on the veranda. Maisie had run ahead to open the door with a wailing of anguished comments that the old man could not make head nor tail of.

'She'll be fine, Pa. It's her shoulder. They've sent for old Maya. I'll take

Helen up to her room.'

'To hear that woman carrying on so, you'd think she'd been stomped to death,' the old man said, turning to Lee Brent.

'The stable door slammed and frightened her horse as she was passing,' the gambler explained.

'Well, let's hope it's none too serious or she'll be mad as a hellcat,' John Ross replied, turning his attention to the ageing Negress who was crossing the yard, with a basket on her arm. Old Maya was respected both by the workers and the Ross family for her skills in dealing with accidents and fevers — of both the animal and human kind.

She could set bones and strap sprains and injuries as well as any doctor and could concoct healing potions and dressings from herbs which she grew in her own fertile patch outside her hut.

'Miss Helen has done her shoulder. She's in her room,' John Ross informed Maya. The old woman hurried into the house to where Helen Ross was being comforted by her husband and a nervous Maisie.

Old Maya scowled at Maisie who found an excuse to make a quick exit. Daniel Ross stepped away from the bed to allow the old woman a closer inspection of his wife.

'Don' fret, Missie Helen. Lie still,' Maya said as she placed her basket on the side table. The old woman's hands explored the injured shoulder. Helen Ross let out a sigh and focused her attention on Maya's seemingly ageless face. Nobody knew how old she was. Her face was unwrinkled, her skin taut across strong bones. Helen Ross felt safe in her hands.

Maya's sensitive fingers traced the problem and she nodded her head in satisfaction.

With Daniel Ross's help she removed Helen's blouse, then, while he followed the old woman's instruction to hold his wife tight, Maya took hold of Helen's arm and shoulder. Without any forewarning, she wrenched it quickly. Helen Ross gave a cry and fainted against her husband.

Ignoring Daniel Ross's glare, the medical woman busied herself with a roll of cloth which she took from her basket. Expertly, she fashioned a sling to support the injured shoulder. Daniel Ross helped Maya to make his wife more comfortable, propping her up againse a pile of pillows.

'She'll be right as rain, Master Daniel,' the old woman said, producing a bottle of salts and passing it under Helen's nose.

Slowly Helen's eyes fluttered open as she began to recover her senses. Maya grunted with satisfaction and proceeded to pour liquid from another of her mysterious bottles into a glass and let Helen Ross sip it. Helen Ross sighed and closed her eyes. Maya eased her back onto the pillows.

'She will feel pain. Maybe a little fever. It will go,' she told Daniel Ross, putting up three fingers, and adding,

'She will be OK after them weeks.'

Checking her basket, Maya made to leave. 'I will come back tomorrow,' she concluded.

'Exactly what was wrong?' Daniel Ross asked.

'It came out. Now it is back,' Maya explained, using her free hand on her own shoulder to indicate the problem. Helen Ross had dislocated her shoulder and it would be three weeks before she could use it again. Maya's treatment and herbal medicine would heal it. Now all Helen Ross had to do was rest.

Pablo Ortiz, having calmed the stallion down after the furore that followed Miss Helen's fall, walked the beautiful animal around the corral. He had never seen such a specimen as this King Cotton. He whispered words of praise as he paused to stroke and inspect the fine lines of the thoroughbred. The horse snorted and lowered his head.

'You are a magnificent animal and

I am a great rider. Together we will work well,' Pablo said, slipping his foot into the left stirrup and lifting his body across the saddle. The stallion's ears perked and he side-stepped towards the fencing. Pablo lay across the saddle, whispering into the horse's ear. Feeling no further movement the horse stood still again, only its ears and eyes showing any reaction.

'There my friend,' Pablo assured, 'I will not harm you.' Leaning close to King Cotton's neck he carried on with his soothing talk as he agilely swung his free leg over the animal's back. Still keeping his head close to King Cotton's ear he tapped his flank and the stallion stepped forward.

The young Mexican straightened himself in the saddle and King Cotton reacted with a snort and a stiff-legged jump. Pablo grinned to himself and, staying firmly glued to the saddle, he pulled the stallion's head round and his heels gently nudged King Cotton's sides. The stallion responded to his urgings and once through the open corral gates, Pablo felt the raw power of the beast as it broke into a fast gallop. The young Mexican allowed the stallion his head as they sped over the broad expanse of the grass meadow. Eventually King Cotton began to slow his pace and the horse and rider cantered for a stretch before Pablo took full control and began to test the stallion's reactions as he varied his signals and commands, changing speed and direction.

King Cotton responded well to the young Mexican's masterly control and, from time to time, Pablo lay low along the stallion's neck to pat and praise him.

After exercising the stallion, Pablo Ortiz cantered towards the stable, unaware that John Ross and Lee Brent had been watching the performance of horse and rider from the house veranda, as they waited for old Maya's report on Helen Ross's condition.

Daniel Ross joined them to tell them

that Helen would be three weeks at least with her arm in a sling. John Ross listened with his eyes on the stallion as it slowed to a walk, entering the corral.

'She won't be able to ride in the Kentucky Races. It's only a month away and she was thinking of riding King Cotton herself, wasn't she?'

His son nodded in agreement. 'Yes. She'll be very disappointed. I suppose we'll have to withdraw King Cotton. There's no one else Helen will let ride him.'

John Ross stood up. 'Leave it for now,' he said and entered the house. It was time for his siesta.

'Missie Helen is fine . . . restin' an fine,' Maisie said from the stairs as Ross crossed to enter his own room on the ground floor.

'Leave her that way, Maisie. Don't go fussing. Sleep's what a good body needs and that includes me.'

'Yes, Master Ross . . . ' Maisie wanted to ask about refreshments, but the old man walked on past her and into his room, closing the door firmly behind him. Lying down on the single bed that had been installed in the room, he smiled to himself.

'That Mex is sure something,' he mused to himself. 'As well as being quite a fighter, he's some rider.' The old man closed his eyes and went off to sleep, picturing the Mexican winning the race at the Kentucky meeting.

8

King Cotton stood still and at ease as Pablo Ortiz chatted to it as he lovingly groomed the stallion.

'You must be good for us both today,' he explained. 'Señora Ross will be watching. Only if you are my good friend will she allow us to work together.' Pablo knew it would not be long before he established a lasting bond with this magnificent beast. With care and dexterity, he saddled the horse and led it out of the stable and into the empty corral. Mounting, he began the exercises that he and the horse had followed daily since Helen Ross had had her accident a week ago.

Helen Ross sat, with her injured shoulder in a sling, on the veranda, watching the young Mexican put her horse through his paces. Finishing the warm-up exercises, Ortiz trotted over

149

to the fence nearest the veranda and dismounted.

'He is my good friend, Señora Ross, yes?' he called across, as he fished a titbit from his pocket and palmed it to King Cotton's muzzle. Helen smiled at the young man's eagerness.

'You treat him well. Don't spoil him or he'll take advantage,' she warned.

'Reward not spoil, Señora Ross. He does good, I say thank you. He not so good, we try again.'

Swinging back into the saddle he made for the opening and Helen watched as the horse and rider gained speed and disappeared over the meadowland.

John Ross had kept his daughter-in-law informed about King Cotton's routine and progress and had suggested that she wait a while before withdrawing the stallion from entry in the Kentucky races. She had agreed, hoping to recover sufficiently, but both she and the plantation owner knew her shoulder would not be strong enough to hold the large thoroughbred. Helen Ross was beginning to consider, what her father-in-law had already decided, that with Ortiz in the saddle King Cotton had a better chance of winning.

When not working with the horses, Ortiz trained with Ezra in the stable. Lee Brent kept an eye on his young friend, making sure he did not overtax himself in his eagerness to prove his abilities both as a rider and a fighter. Often the only sounds the gambler could hear as he wandered into the stable were the muffled thuds of Pablo's fists punching the heavy bag or the more human grunts of both Ezra and the young Mexican as they sparred.

Lee Brent had had a word with John Ross about changing the venue for the fight and, although he was noncommittal, the shrewd plantation owner could see the sense in providing a larger arena for the Mexican to fight in.

'Leave it with me. I'll talk to the others,' he had promised.

Lee Brent often rode into Rossville to follow his chosen profession, playing cards in the saloons. In town, he listened to the local gossip and chit-chat. The Dutchman's name was mentioned often and his followers bragged about what Larson would do to the next fighter from the Ross plantation, whenever the gambler was within earshot. Brent smiled wryly at their comments and would not be drawn into any discussion.

Alvin Hughes came into the saloon one day whilst Brent was playing a game of poker. He stood watching the gambler, his man Brock, as usual, at his elbow, his gloved hand close to his low-slung .45. Brock's cold eyes watched Brent as he picked up the pot of money before him.

The gambler felt the hostile stare and momentarily looked up before returning his attention to the fresh cards that landed in front of him. He picked them up and studied them, his face immobile as he asked for two cards. Picking them up, he discarded two from his hand. Brock's eyes were still on him. Brent looked over his hand before placing the cards, face down, on the table, and lifting his gaze to study both Hughes and his henchman.

'Is there something I can do for you, gentlemen?' Brent asked.

Brock's hand touched his gun as Hughes spoke. 'I hear you're staying at the Ross plantation.'

Brent kept his attention on Brock as he replied to Hughes's questioning. 'Does it matter to you, where I stay?' he asked.

'Mister Hughes asked you a question.' Brock's hand closed over his .45. The gambler's right hand slid inside his coat.

'Leave it, Brock,' Hughes said. 'We don't want to fall out with Mr Ross's visitor. How is your friend, the Mex?'

So that's what it's all about, thought Brent. They must have heard about Pablo Ortiz and his work-outs with Ezra. It had been plantation gossip for awhile now and was bound to have spread to the town. The gambler placed both hands back on the table and decided to play dumb.

'What about the Mexican?' he countered.

'They say he's some fighter,' Hughes persisted.

'Who says?' the gambler continued and, picking up his cards, added, 'Now if you will excuse me, gentlemen, I have a living to make.' With that, Brent turned his attention to the game in hand and seemingly ignored both Hughes and his foreman. His apparent show of indifference was only a bluff. He could see that Brock was a dangerous man. His cold look had sent a warning tremor down the gambler's spine. He had met men like Brock before and Brent suspected that Hughes was the type of man who would have no qualms in using the born-killer's skills if he felt it necessary.

Getting no answers to his queries, Hughes impatiently motioned Brock and they left the table.

'If the jawing's true, this Mex must be something, the way they are keeping him undercover. Let's go see what all the talk is about. By the way, the gambler's carrying a shoulder holster.'

Brock nodded, 'I noticed, boss. There's no danger there.' Hughes made no further comment as they left the saloon and mounted their horses, but he had not seen any fear on Lee Brent's face. Taking the plantation road out of town, Alvin Hughes decided to pay a personal visit to John Ross, to check out the Mexican, using the excuse that he wanted to see how the young fighter Mose was faring after his fight with the Dutchman.

Hughes and his hired gunny pulled up outside the Ross main building. Helen Ross made to rise from her seat on the veranda.

'You stay comfortable, Helen. I heard you had a fall. Hope you're feeling a mite improved,' the rancher called as he dismounted, passed the reins to his foreman and stepped towards the veranda, keeping the broad expanse of the yard and corral in sight.

Helen Ross replied with cool courtesy and asked if she could be of any help.

'I'm looking for John Ross. Is he in?' Hughes asked. 'Thing is, I came to enquire after his boy — the one that was hurt fighting my man — wondered if he's recovered enough to contemplate Larson again.'

Hughes's eyes searched about and from his horse Brock scanned further afield.

'He's around somewhere. Ezra might know,' Helen Ross replied pleasantly, nodding towards the stables.

Hughes was pleased with the answer. It gave him the opportunity to take a look around and possibly find out more about this Mexican for himself. Thanking Helen Ross, he made his way to the stables. A young Negro was busy tossing hay into a stall.

Hughes called out, 'Is Ezra or Mr Ross here-abouts?'

'No, sir, Master John and Master Daniel is out inspectin' and Ezra's with the horses.' The boy paused and waited for further questions.

'Where's the Mex?' Hughes asked.

'Him out riding Missie Helen's horse.'

Hughes spotted the hanging bag as he looked about.

'Mose back in training?' he questioned.

'No, sir. Mose's fightin' days over,' the boy answered, bug-eyed.

'You mean Ezra's got no fighter to train?'

'Sure has,' the youngster said, creasing up with laughter. 'That Mexican keep Ezra busy, busy busy.'

Alvin Hughes feigned humour. 'The word in town is that he's some fighter.'

The young Negro's face became serious again. 'Yessir, yessiree, that man is one tornado.'

Alvin Hughes left the stables and beckoned to Brock to join him as he walked round the buildings to the corral where Ezra was tending to a couple of mares with their foals. The big Negro straightened himself to his full height as he watched Hughes walk over to him.

The ranch owner noticed Ezra's freshly swollen features. If the Mex was responsible for the damage, he must be something special. Hughes leaned on the fence and scrutinized both the man and the animals. 'Some fine critters you got there, Ezra.'

It was while he was speaking to Ezra that the young Mexican rode in. Hughes stood watching his horsemanship. Entering the corral, Pablo Ortiz jumped down lightly from the back of the big stallion and moved forward to stroke and pat its face and neck before leading it towards the stables. The easy way Ortiz handled the horse impressed the rancher and he studied the young Mexican as he controlled the big thoroughbred.

He was tall for a Mex — well muscled, stocky built and agile as a mountain cat.

Pablo Ortiz called to Ezra that he would tend to King Cotton and carried on into the stables, ignoring the visitors.

Hughes gambled on surprising Ezra. 'Who's the new wrangler? Got to hand it to him, the way he handles that there highbrow horse, something none of my boys'd entertain. I heard you got a new hand and talk is, he's quite a fighter.'

If Ezra was taken by surprise he didn't show it, answering, 'I only know Mr John has hired him to ride Miss Helen's horse. She got hurt in a fall.' The big man said no more and went on tending the animals, hoping Hughes would leave him alone. The rancher turned to where Brock and the horses were patiently waiting and, remounting, swung round to face the big house on his way to find the plantation owner. He walked his horse in silence, grimacing to himself. There was something going on here. He knew old Ross for a sly old varmint. The Mex looked good but not in the same stable as Larson, he deduced.

Hughes pulled to a halt, having spotted John Ross and his son heading back along the plantation road towards the house, and then slowly made his way over in his direction. John Ross saw him coming.

'We have a surprise visitor,' he remarked to his son.

Hughes extended his hand across the pommel as they met. 'You're looking well, John. How's your boy? Is he recovering?'

John Ross nodded. 'It'll take time but he'll recover,' he said, and waited for more questions.

'Thing is, we need to start thinking of the arrangements for the next fight. The boys in town keep asking questions.'

'Come on up to the house,' the old man said, clicking his horse on. 'I, for one, need a long drink and I'm sure you do, too.'

'I won't keep you long, John,' Hughes

persisted, as the four walked their horses on towards the main building 'Just wondered if you had anybody else lined up for the Dutchman?'

'Possibly,' Ross answered. 'I'll let you know after the Kentucky meeting. I could have somebody ready by then. Ezra has his eye on one or two of the workers.'

'Saw your Mex wrangler in the corral, just now. Looks handy, if he was a bit bigger,' Hughes ventured.

John Ross wrinkled his nose at the suggestion. 'I don't think so. We brought him in to ride King Cotton when Helen got hurt. If you want a good bet for the Kentucky meet, you could do worse.'

'Thanks, John, I'll remember that.'

At that moment Maisie came out of the house to shrill to John Ross that coffee and refreshments were ready.

'You'll join us for a bite?' John Ross asked the rancher.

'No thanks, John. I just called in to see how your man, Mose, was faring.

I've other business to attend to.'

John Ross watched his visitors leave with a wry smile on his face.

'That old twister has something up his sleeve,' Hughes told his henchman.

'Could be bluffin' boss. Whatever it is it won't bother the Dutchman none,' Brock retorted.

Hughes agreed but he sensed that the old plantation owner had something brewing and Hughes intended to find out exactly what it was.

It was three weeks to the Kentucky meeting. Hughes made further enquiries in town about the Mexican but could find no one to confirm what the young stableboy at the Ross plantation had told him.

The week for the Kentucky Race Meeting arrived. Pablo Ortiz had done his work well with King Cotton. The horse was in perfect condition and Helen Ross, having watched the progress between man and beast had, to Pablo's delight, asked her father-in-law if he could ride him. After some feigned deliberation and coaxing, John Ross agreed.

The fees charged for the entries made up the purse which would be presented in total to the winner. Many side bets were made between individuals and a lot of money was placed on the plantation entry, King Cotton. Lee Brent, Alvin Hughes and all the owners including the Ross family, were high stakers and most of Rossville's population had a flutter.

There were ten horses in the race and it was while Brent and Ortiz were going down the list of owners and runners that the gambler read out the name of Don Felipe Lopez. Pablo Ortiz, who up till then had felt restlessly nervous about the race, drew in his breath before cursing out loud, in his own tongue. The gambler was taken aback.

'What's wrong?' he enquired. Pablo stabbed his finger at the name of Don Felipe Lopez.

'That was my *patron* — Don Felipe Lopez. The one who beat me. The one who listened to the lies of his daughter.'

The young Mexican's back stiffened and his eyes searched the gathering of people looking for the don among the crowd of owners, racegoers, carriages and horses as they mingled together. He saw no one he knew from the Lopez *hacienda*.

The time of the race arrived. The setting became more orderly. The horses and riders were called to take their places. Ortiz swung aboard the stallion with last-minute instructions whispered in his ear by an anxious Ezra.

'Go for it, Pablo. Run for the line,' Lee Brent urged.

'You know what to do. Win for Missie Helen. Good luck,' Ezra called, as Daniel Ross led the horse and rider to join the others.

Pablo's face set in concentration. He would race to beat Don Felipe Lopez. King Cotton would race for Señora Helen. How could they lose?

9

The parade gave the crowd a last chance to view the horses and riders who were to take part in the Kentucky race. Joining the runners as they circled the area, Pablo Ortiz soon spotted the mount and rider being led in by Pedro Gomez, his old *caporal*. Don Felipe's rider was a slim-built Mexican. The *hacendado* had obviously gone for a lightweight, hoping it would give his rider an advantage. Pedro Gomez was too involved giving last-minute instructions to the rider to notice Ortiz, but Pablo hoped to have a word with him, later. First he must win the race.

The horses lined up at the start. King Cotton seemed to understand what was expected of him. With his ears pricked and pointed, his head straining forward, the stallion was eager to be off. All eyes focused on the raised flag as a silence fell over the meeting. When it dropped, the crowd roared and the horses took off. Pablo's booted heels stroked the stallion's sides as it surged forward among the leaders. Crouching low over its neck, his familiar voice urged the animal on. King Cotton's powerful frame responded. The expertise of Pablo Ortiz was there for all to see as he guided John Ross's horse ahead of all his adversaries to win the race with a length to spare.

The crowd went wild as the winner was formally announced and the young Mexican warmed to the applause as the horse and rider became the centre of attention. A beaming Ezra held King Cotton steady as the Ross family pushed their way forward to congratulate their rider. Helen Ross was the picture of happiness as she raised a gloved hand to the young Mexican.

'You did well, Pablo. You both did well,' she said. John Ross joined them, smiling. That was the first part of the double this young Mexican was going to win for him. The clincher would be licking the Dutchman.

An angry cry from the perimeter of the circle of well-wishers, interrupted their congratulations. The plantation owner looked over enquiringly, wondering what the commotion was about. He saw the well-dressed *hacendado*, whom he recognized as the owner of the horse that had come in second behind the Ross stallion, gesticulating angrily towards Ortiz. John Ross thought he was protesting about the race as he advanced, whip in hand. through the hurriedly dividing crowd. A young woman hurried along behind him, closely followed by a middle-aged Mexican. In his native tongue, the *hacendado*, was furiously cursing the young winner. From what John Ross could make out, with his scant knowledge of the language, his rider was supposed to be dead. He also seemed to be accusing Pablo Qrtiz of molesting his daughter.

Pablo Ortiz swung down from King Cotton and moved away from his astonished group of well-wishers. The young Mexican took a stance as his ex-*patron* came towards him and, with his head held high, vehemently denied the stream of accusations.

Catching up with his *patron*, the middle-aged Mexican stopped in his tracks. Pedro Gomez was so surprised to see Pablo Ortiz that, for a moment, he was speechless. Suddenly, Don Felipe's anger peaked and, raising the whip, he stepped forward to deliver a blow.

The night of his whipping came flooding back to the young Mexican. Pablo Ortiz recalled the pain as he lay defenceless as his *patron* lashed him unmercifully before leaving him for dead. Never again! Pablo's left hand flashed up to catch the whip before it connected. Swinging the patron's arm to one side, he lashed out with his right fist, smashing it into the face of the don. The sound could be heard around the gathered circle of people. Gasps echoed out as Don Felipe thudded to the ground and lay still. Pablo Ortiz snatched the whip from his grip and raised it above the crumpled body.

It was Pedro Gomez who sprang forward, to kneel alongside the body of his fallen *patron*. The whip lashed down across Pedro's head and shoulders as Ortiz, temporarily blind with rage, struck at his prostrate tormentor, Don Felipe. Pedro Gomez winced in pain as he covered his *patron*'s body with his own and his cries urgently begged Ortiz to stop. The red mist cleared and the young Mexican let the whip drop from his grasp.

John Ross took charge of the situation and persuaded the gathering crowd to disperse. 'Nothing to worry about folks. Your winnings are safe. Give the horses and riders some space. Just a private misunderstanding. We'll deal with the problem in a proper manner.'

People drifted away leaving the fallen Don Felipe surrounded by his

169

daughter, his *caporal* and members of the Ross party to resolve the matter. Maria Lopez knelt sobbing at her father's side, watching Gomez as he attempted to bring her father back to consciousness. Glancing up at Ortiz, who stood off to one side, still angry but restrained, she bemoaned his attack on her father, calling him evil and berating him savagely.

The young Mexican waited for her tirade to end, his eyes fixed on the now recovering *hacendado* before he once again voiced his protest. This time his tone was low, even and in deadly earnest.

'I will not be punished twice for something I did not do even once. The *señorita* did not tell the truth,' he declared.

Don Felipe shook himself free from the ministrations of his *caporal*.

'You told me he was dead,' he accused, struggling to his feet. Pointing a finger at Pablo Ortiz, he continued, 'You dare to call my daughter a liar.

You are less than vermin.'

Pedro Gomez wearily grabbed at his *patron*'s arm. His face was crestfallen for he knew that what he was about to say would mean the end of his employment on the *hacienda*.

'Pablo Ortiz speaks the truth, my *patron*. I was there. I saw what happened,' he said, slowly but clearly. Don Felipe could not and would not believe what he was hearing. Furiously, he turned away as his daughter cried out hysterically and ran from the scene. Don Felipe seethed inside. His name had been dishonoured. He would not forget the people responsible. He picked up the fallen whip and lashed Gomez across the side of the head with it.

'You have both insulted my family. If I see either of you again, I will have you shot,' he said before storming off angrily after his daughter.

Pablo Ortiz studied the don's old *caporal*, 'You knew I did not molest the *señorita*?'

Gomez hung his head and nodded.

'Is that why you helped me to escape?'

'It is,' Gomez replied. 'I told the don that you were dead and that I had buried your body.'

Ortiz could not be angry with Gomez. Knowing the way of life in Mexico, Pablo knew Gomez would have endangered his own livelihood if he had spoken out against the word of the don's daughter. He had had to keep quiet about what he had seen and under the circumstances Gomez had done the best he could for Ortiz after his beating and the young Mexican knew he owed him his life.

John Ross placed his hand on Pablo's shoulder. He had heard most of the words that had been spoken and had gleaned the full story.

'Don't let that highfalutin *hacendado* spoil our day. Guess he's just riled to think you won,' he said, dismissing the incident. 'Time to get King Cotton over to the Louisville stables. Your friend there can give you and Ezra a

172

hand if he likes,' he added, walking back to join his group, with a satisfied grin. This young Mexican was quite a horseman and after seeing the way he defended himself against the angry don, John Ross intended employing him for as long as the young firebrand would stay. The older Mexican too, if he wished. There was always room for a good *vaquero*.

A keen observer of the confrontation between the Mexicans and the *hacendado* had been Alvin Hughes. Deep down something was beginning to niggle and worry him. He had seen the young Mexican defend himself against the *hacendado*, showing no deference to his social superior. Hughes began to suspect that he could lose a lot of money if the Mex showed such disregard towards his Dutchman. He turned to his hired gunny.

'That dandified greaser might have done us a favour, threatening to kill Ross's rider. If the Mex was to get shot, we'd have somebody to blame.'

Brock's hand brushed his .45. 'Just say the word,' he growled.

'Let's leave it for a while, till it suits us,' said Hughes, as the two men strolled past the plantation owner.

'Congratulations, John. I did as you advised and backed your horse and rider. He's quite a horseman.' Lingering only long enough to remark on how well Helen Ross looked, Hughes nodded to all and went to claim his winnings from his wager.

After the celebrations, John Ross, his son and wife made their way to their hotel where they were later joined by Lee Brent, who had had a very lucrative day, one way and another, and was also a happy winner. John Ross told him briefly about Ortiz and the *hacendado*.

'Where is Pablo? I've something to cheer him up,' the gambler said.

'I think he's had enough excitement for one day, Mr Brent. He's probably curled up fast asleep within a nose of King Cotton,' Helen Ross laughed.

Her comment was furthest from the truth. Over in the Louisville stables, Ortiz and Ezra were wide awake, telling Gomez all about the young Mexican's recent past and his hopes for the future. Pedro Gomez listened with wet eyes. He had often wondered what had happened to the handsome young *remudero*.

Ezra, Ortiz and Gomez stayed with the horse till the next day when the long trip home started. The plantation was soon buzzing with excitement as the workers prepared for their own celebrations. Only the most necessary chores were attended to.

John Ross, his son and daughter-in-law hosted the events which lasted best part of the day and into the evening. The children of the workers took part in the afternoon activities, racing and picnicking, and later the owners were entertained by the singing and music volunteered by some of their workers.

The next morning, everything was back to normal. The daily routines were followed as if nothing had happened at all. The Rosses were in eagle-eyed control and no allowance was expected or given for the previous evening's late hours and frantic activities.

★ ★ ★

Pedro Gomez had been relieved to have been offered a job and the chance to work, once again, with the young *remudero*. A spare cot had been added to the room above the stable — a slight inconvenience Ezra had preferred to Mabel's offer to share her hut, next to the laundry.

Gomez soon settled in, helping to look after the quarter horses, the Morgans and the Walkers, which Daniel Ross used on plantation inspections, as well as the thoroughbreds, once Señora Helen had seen how proficient he was. Having Gomez around to help gave Ezra more time to spend with the young Mexican. They followed their training schedule daily without interruption, watched from time to time by the gambler and the old plantation owner, who was well satisfied with what he saw.

'Reckon it's time,' he said to Brent, one morning as they left the stables.

John Ross sent word to Alvin Hughes to call a meeting in town to arrange the fight.

This was duly arranged and a few days later, John Ross, accompanied by Lee Brent, entered the town hotel to find the rancher and his sidekick already waiting with the rest of the interested party of businessmen for his arrival.

'Well, John, see you made it. Thought you were going to chicken out there for a while,' Hughes bantered, eyeing his timepiece. 'Sit yourself down and tell us what we're all waiting to hear. Who have you got to fight my man this time? Another Black?'

John Ross took his time settling himself down on the proffered seat.

'Don't play coy with me, Alvin. I

think you've suspected all along who it is. I hope you had a side wager on it. If you bet it would be the Mexican you're in the money. Reckon most of the townsfolk did.'

One or two of the others in the company laughed at Hughes's obvious discomfort.

'I didn't think he would be big enough,' Hughes scowled.

'He's big enough and good enough,' Ross replied evenly.

The old man was too confident and Alvin Hughes was worried.

'When do you want the *Mississippi Queen*?' Captain Turner, who had also been invited, asked.

'I didn't intend using your boat, this time, Turner. I thought a building on land somewhere,' the old plantation owner answered, waiting in the following silence to see what Hughes's reaction would be.

Some of the businessmen voiced their disapproval. If it was held on land, there was the chance of the townswomen's guild getting wind of it and putting a stop to any influx of Turner's 'soiled doves', into Rossville. They saw their after-fight pleasures being thwarted.

'There's no place in town suitable or big enough,' Hughes added.

'And my boat's been the venue for many a fight, Mr Ross. It's part of my living, so to speak,' interrupted the captain.

'I could clear out one of my store barns,' Ross suggested. 'Also, the women you gents are worried about, can be accommodated on the paddler and the captain will, as always, supply your needs both culinary and otherwise for a small fee.'

The men laughed self-consciously.

'Why change the venue?' Hughes countered. 'What's wrong with the *Mississippi Queen*?'

'Nothing. Nothing at all,' John Ross replied coolly. 'But the last time my fighter was on board he was threatened with being thrown overboard. The simple matter is he can't swim. Even thinking about it makes him nervous. Getting him on board would seem to put him at a disadvantage, Alvin, and I'm sure you wouldn't want that. Truth is, he won't go on board a boat, for whatever reason, which if you don't agree to change the venue means there'll be no fight.'

The others saw the possibility of their prospective entertainment disappearing and eagerly began to accommodate the alternative suggestion. After all, a fight on land, followed by a night of food, drink and revelry sounded very enticing and they hastened to assure Captain Turner that neither he nor his ladies would suffer any monetary loss.

The rancher kept a scowl on his face, although he knew that if he played his cards right, John Ross would have to consider his next proposal, and Alvin Hughes had an ace up his sleeve. Hughes listened sulkily while the rest of them concluded that if John Ross could fix things they would be agreeable.

'Only one thing bothers me about such a venue,' Alvin Hughes spoke up. 'Who's to say that Mex won't hightail it at the last minute? On the *Mississippi Queen* he'd have had nowhere to go, if what you say's true about him being 'fraid of water. What if he gets scared of the Dutchman? Between me and you, John, what would you say to 'winner take all' if one of the fighters doesn't appear?'

John Ross frowned at the rancher's suggestion. He suspected Hughes was up to something, but he couldn't think what. The plantation owner was tempted to abandon the whole thing.

'I don't know,' he stalled. Lee Brent whispered to him and the two men excused themselves to confer in private.

'What's the problem, Mr Ross? Accept the wager. Nothing's going to stop Pablo from being there. I will stay closer to Ortiz than his shirt. If Hughes and his sidekick have got anything in mind, Ezra, Gomez and the rest of the crew will be on the alert.'

John Ross returned to the table and formally agreed to the wager with a firm shake of Hughes's hand. The fight would be in two weeks' time.

10

Once the town's business men had got used to the idea of the new venue being sited on land down by the docking area, a buzz of activity ensued. John Ross became engrossed in organizing the emptying of one of his storage barns and fitting it out with tables and chairs, making sure that the central area, which was to be the ring, was the suggested size laid down by the young Mexican.

'We can get more tables in if we move them closer, Mr Ross,' one of his workers suggested.

'No. That'll do fine,' the old man affirmed. 'Give them a bit of space to move around.'

When he was satisfied that all was as it should be, John Ross asked Lee Brent to bring the Mexican to the barn to give his opinion. The plantation owner was quite surprised when Lee Brent arrived with Pablo, Pedro and Ezra.

'Pablo reckons he needs to get the feel of the place,' the gambler explained.

'If we could have a little privacy . . . ' he added, nodding towards the couple of workers still in the barn.

'Oh, sure,' John Ross answered, dismissing them.

Lee Brent took a seat at one of the tables and the old plantation owner joined him. They watched as the young Mexican paced around the central area before beginning a routine of shadowboxing that took him forward, backwards and sideways as he displayed a series of punches designed to confuse his invisible opponent with their speed and change of direction. His workout continued without slackening of pace as he criss-crossed the designated area displaying light-balanced footwork and a variety of punches, jabs, crosses and uppercuts.

Stopping only to invite Ezra to join him, Pablo pulled off his shirt and took a stance in the middle of the ring. Ezra smiled as he moved slowly through the tables with Pedro Gomez close behind him.

'Just remember, the Dutchman may be slower on his feet than you but he can move faster than I can,' the big Negro reminded Ortiz as he joined the young Mexican.

They began to spar, with Ortiz circling, darting and closing in on the stolid, defensive Ezra. The Negro's cover was sound and the young Mexican had his work cut out as the session developed. Both fighters were loath to finish when John Ross called a halt.

'You'd better save some of that for the Dutchman,' he observed, before asking, 'Is the ring to your satisfaction?'

'*Si*, Señor Ross.' Pablo exhaled heavily, adding with a grin, 'I think this will do very well for me but not so well for the Dutchman.'

'I think it will do very well for us all,' Lee Brent added.

Pedro Gomez handed Pablo his shirt and the young man wiped his sweating torso with it before pulling it back on.

'Well, if you're satisfied, I certainly am,' John Ross concluded. 'Just take it easy and keep out of sight. Make sure he gets his sleep and good vittles, Ezra. Looks like you're doing a good job with him.'

'I sure will, Mr Ross. Thank you, sir,' Ezra said with a beaming smile of pride as he joined the two Mexicans leaving the barn.

Pablo Ortiz was delighted with the bigger ring space that he knew would give him an advantage over the lumbering Dutchman. He attacked his training with renewed verve and worked very hard with Ezra, in the stables. Once his sparring and floor exercising was over he would join Pedro Gomez on a lengthy trot and run routine which took them through part of the plantation area. Ezra would watch them go and retire for a spell before resuming his chores. The Negro was pleased with the young Mexican's progress. His punching, already awesome, was now more so. Pablo Ortiz was reaching his full potential. It was going to be some fight.

Three days before the day of the fight, Ortiz and Gomez were trotting and running along the roads that wound their way through the plantation. Gomez had settled in well and was pleased that he had renewed his friendship with young Ortiz. The horror of the past was dimming in both their memories and was replaced by a pride they both shared in being Mexican. Pablo Ortiz teased the older man about how he would consider giving him a job on his *hacienda* when he had received his winnings from the fight.

'Of course, I will have to see if you are worthy to look after my horses, *señor*. You may be too old,' the young Mexican bantered as he speeded up, shooting away from his companion.

Pedro Gomez found he could not retort and run at the same time so he trotted on doggedly, muttering behind clenched teeth. As he rounded a corner, he was pounced on by a shrieking Ortiz who had been lying in wait for him. They cavorted like children before slowing down to a walking pace. Getting his breath back, Gomez resumed the banter, telling Ortiz that counting chickens was a foolish man's game and that perhaps he, Pedro Gomez, would be the one offering the job. After all he was a *caporal* and Ortiz was only a *remudero*.

'But I am a fighting *remudero*. Can you fight, *Caporal*?' Ortiz challenged, striking a pose in front of his companion.

Gomez jumped forward and grabbed the young Mexican by the forearms. Ortiz reacted, exerting pressure to one side, spinning them both around.

It was at that moment that a shot rang out. Pedro Gomez tightened then released his hold on Pablo's arms and slowly slid down into a heap at the young Mexican's feet. Letting out an involuntary cry, Pablo Ortiz stumbled backward, his eyes searching in the direction from whence the sound had come. He saw a man rise up from a clump of bushes and vanish into the trees behind him. In his hand was a rifle. Suddenly aware that he too was in danger, he dodged behind the nearest cotton bush and waited. The sound of a horse racing away in the distance came to the young Mexican's ears and, when the sound finally died away, Ortiz left his cover and stooped over the body of the fallen *caporal*. Slowly he dropped to his knees.

'Señor Gomez . . . *Caporal*,' he whispered but there was no reply. Ortiz struggled to ease his strong, young arm under his companion's back to lift him into a sitting position. A hot, sticky warmth enveloped his fingers as blood oozed from Gomez's back. Ortiz studied the face of his old *caporal*. The shot had been fatal. Gently he laid his dead companion back on the ground and got to his feet. Spurred by grief and anger and heedless of danger, he ran swiftly over to the bushes from whence the shot had come. He could see where the gunman had lain in wait. The grass was flattened, twigs had been broken where the bushwhacker had made a gap to observe the road. By the look of it he had lain in wait for a long spell. Ortiz searched the area. A silver object glittered and caught his eye. He picked it up. It was a silver concho, worn mostly by Mexicans for decoration. It must have fallen from the clothing or belt of the man who had fired the shot, Ortiz decided. The threat to kill him from Don Felipe came to mind. He looked towards the prostrate form of Gomez. If he had not pulled his old *caporal* around as they fooled about, it would have been himself, Pablo Ortiz, who would be lying there. The bushwhacker had been intending to kill him.

The young Mexican looked around

before slowly following the boot prints of the gunman, plainly evident in the ground. He came to the trees and found the place where the bushwhacker's horse had been tethered. The ground was disturbed and it was evident that the animal had been there for a good while. The man must have known the area and Ortiz's habit of using the paths for his road exercises. He would go back to talk to Lee Brent and John Ross; perhaps they would be able to shed some light on who it could possibly be. Gomez's killer would have to be found.

Ortiz studied the silver concho in his hand. If it was a Mexican who had done the shooting, Don Felipe would be the antagonist. He, Ortiz, would take his revenge if it was proved to be so. Returning to the prostrate form of his companion, Ortiz removed his own shirt and laid it over Pedro Gomez's face.

'I am sorry my friend . . . ' he began, before a lump in his throat silenced him. Turning homewards he set off at an ever-increasing speed to arrive at the stable shirtless, breathless and distressed.

Seeing his tearstained face, Ezra knew there was something wrong.

'Where is Pedro? What has happened?' he asked, as Pablo fought to get his breath.

'He . . . is . . . dead. Bushwhacked. I think . . . the bullet was meant . . . for me.'

'What you saying? Sit down and get your wind back while I go tell Mr Ross,' Ezra said, making for the doorway.

Ezra hobbled across to the big house to tell John Ross about the shooting. The old plantation owner showed concern at the news, concern that Ortiz was uninjured. Ezra assured him he was.

'Better take a couple of horses and go and bring the old Mexican back. Tell young Ortiz to come over and fill me in with the details,' Ross said.

By the time Ezra had got two horses saddled up, Pablo Ortiz had regained his composure and insisted on accompanying the Negro to retrieve Gomez's body before following John Ross's instructions. The two horsemen rode off, with Ortiz taking the lead. Arriving at the spot where Gomez lay, they both dismounted and silently, working together, they hoisted the dead Mexican across the saddle of one of the horses and secured the body. When that was done, Pablo nodded to Ezra and set off walking the corpse-laden horse while Ezra watched him for a while before remounting. When they reached the stables, Pablo handed the reins to Ezra and set off for the main building, where the old man was patiently waiting.

With a voice devoid of emotion, he told John Ross what had happened and about finding the silver concho. Ross raised his eyebrows in surprise. He had for a moment thought it might have been Hughes's work. It was not beyond the rancher's capabilities to have tried to scare off the young Mexican — the bet being as it was about one or other of the contestants not turning up for the fight — but would Hughes have stooped that low, Ross wondered? The finding of the silver concho seemed to indicate that the gunman was of Mexican origin. He recalled that the *hacendado*, Don Felipe Lopez, had made a threat to both the Mexicans. Had he tried to carry it out?

The plantation owner called for some refreshments and sent for Ezra before addressing the young Mexican.

'You sit there a spell and regain your composure. Maisie'll be along with somethin' appetizin' and when the time's right we'll sort this thing out. For now, I want you to concentrate on the business in hand: beating that big Dutchman of Hughes.' When Ezra arrived, John Ross took him to one side and told him to bury Gomez and to make sure that Ortiz stayed indoors until the fight was over. When the Negro went to interrupt, the plantation owner pointed out that the young Mexican needed to be kept calm and not be reminded of the death of his *compadre*, that he needed to concentrate on the matter in hand, namely the fight.

'After all, his future depends on it, doesn't it?' he added. A comment that Ezra could not disagree with. After the fight, he, John Ross would help the young Mexican to find out who had killed his friend.

★ ★ ★

Brock rode into the Rolling H yard. Taking the Winchester from the saddle scabbard, he called to old Jake, the wrangler, to take care of his mount. Head down and scowling, Brock headed for the ranch house, knocked and entered. Alvin Hughes came from the back room to welcome his foreman, having watched him ride in, through the back window. The look on Brock's face told him that he had failed on the

195

job he had sent him out to do. Brock tossed his rifle onto the side table.

'Well?' Hughes said, waiting for an answer.

'I missed him. The other Mex got in the way.'

Hughes let out a curse. Brock was a first-class shot. Before he could question him further, his foreman told him what had happened.

'Did you leave the concho?' Hughes asked him.

'Yes.'

'Well, that should make them think it's the dandified greaser carrying out his threat.'

Alvin Hughes handed Brock a bottle of whiskey and a glass. His foreman took it and poured himself a good slug.

'They'll be on their toes over at the plantation from now on, unless the Mex gets cold feet,' the rancher deduced. 'It looks like the fight will go ahead as scheduled. It up to Larson now to do what he's paid to do.'

Hughes took the bottle from Brock and poured himself a stiff drink. He cursed himself for doing such a foolish thing in the first place. After all, the Dutchman should beat the little Mex upstart. But there was a niggle at the back of the rancher's mind. The scene at the racecourse came to mind: the quickness and power of the Mexican's punch that had felled the horse owner. Hughes took a deep swallow. Then again, the Mexican dandy was not the Dutchman. Larson could absorb punches. After another whiskey, Hughes could not see Larson losing the fight.

★ ★ ★

Lee Brent showed concern and surprise when he returned to the Ross plantation and heard the news of the shooting. Looking at the silver concho, he deduced — as Ortiz and the plantation owner had done — that it could have been the work of Don Felipe. But how did the bushwhacker know where Ortiz would be at that time? Not being able to come up with a satisfactory solution the gambler consoled himself with the fact that at least Ortiz had not been injured.

Sorry as both Lee Brent and John Ross were about the death of Gomez, the killing of Pablo Ortiz would have been a greater loss to the plantation owner's bank balance as well as to the fortunes of Lee Brent, who intended to back all his money on his young Mexican friend.

11

The day of the big fight arrived and Lee Brent, together with Ezra and the plantation owner and his son, escorted Pablo Ortiz to the venue in the large storage barn. The tables and chairs circling the central roped-off space were all occupied by the special guests, and others were sorting themselves out as they swapped places and jostled for the next best viewing seats. Over it all the banter and humour rang out, mixed with greetings and the making of private bets. Captain Turner made his flamboyant entrance answering questions about refreshments of one kind and another as he made his way to his seat at the front. Laughter followed his progress and comments and the mood of the crowd heightened.

Alvin Hughes arrived with the

Dutchman and Brock, whose expressionless gaze swept the crowd, ready and alert for any sign of trouble. Hughes was shocked to find that the ring was bigger than he had expected and the rancher pushed his way through to the plantation owner to complain. Hughes wanted it made smaller, but Ross refused and said that if the rancher was not happy he should call the fight off and reminded him that the Mexican would automatically be declared the winner. Hughes turned to see what the Dutchman's reaction was, but Larson did not seem in the least perturbed so the rancher abandoned his protest and both contestants went to get ready for the fight.

At the sight of the two fighters, the crowd centred their concentration and conversation on their relative weight and experience. Some mentioned the young Mexican's recent confrontation with the Mexican don, at the Kentucky meeting, whilst others argued that his opponent had been elderly and cited the Dutchman's ability in the face of all that had been put against him in the past and recalled his last contest with the Ross plantation fighter. Arguments, about youth and vitality against age and experience, the known against the unknown, were raised and considered and eventually each man made his decision. Most of the betting money was placed on the big Dutchman and Lee Brent was kept busy covering most of the bets.

The time came for the contest to begin and the crowd quietened when Captain Turner, who was once again elected as the timekeeper, took his place in the centre of the ring. Praising the venue and reminding the audience of the pleasures available on board the *Mississippi Queen* — where they could commiserate or celebrate — after the fight, he went over the rules of combat before calling for the contestants.

Larson was first to be announced and all heads turned as the massive Dutchman made his way to the central area with Hughes and Brock in close attendance. The crowd muttered their approval. Larson looked in excellent condition, his body gleaming with sweat after his warm-up. Their wagers looked safe.

When Pablo Ortiz made his appearance, walking behind the slow moving Ezra, their reception was more subdued. The young Mexican looked about him with ease. He noticed Lee Brent sitting at the ringside with the old plantation owner and gave his friend a cursory nod.

John Ross was studying his fighter and was pleased with what he saw for, although the muscled body of Pablo Ortiz looked less impressive against the bulk of the Dutchman, there was something about the young Mexican that was threatening.

Pablo Ortiz glanced across the ring at the Dutchman before swinging his gaze to Hughes and Brock, who stood beside him. Ortiz looked into the gunman's cold eyes and the two men locked stares. It was Brock who dropped his eyes momentarily before looking back to find Ortiz was still staring at him. Brock bristled and muttered something to Hughes but the rancher quieted him and continued to instruct his fighter as he rubbed the Dutchman down.

Pablo Ortiz switched his attention to what Ezra was saying.

'You sure got plenty of room to fight here. It's what you ask' for, so keep movin',' he urged.

Pablo Ortiz nodded.

The steamboat captain called both fighters from their corners, to toe the line, and reminded them of the rules before instructing them to defend themselves and hurrying out of the roped-off area, to his ringside seat.

Wasting no time, the Dutchman lunged forward, his hands up, head low. He was brought up short when Ortiz met him with a right uppercut that found its way between Larson's fists. The Dutchman's head jolted back and the huge legs wobbled. Then a left hook swung in as Ortiz, his full weight behind his left shoulder, powered forward again. The crack of the punch rang out as his fist struck home. The big bulk before him staggered and fell back. Larson hit the ground with a heaving shudder, then rolled over on to his stomach. Slowly he climbed to his hands and knees before keeling over on to his side. Captain Turner stepped into the ring and pushed Ortiz to his corner, while Hughes rushed to Larson's side with a dripping cloth, soaked in water, which he wrapped around the Dutchman's head. The captain, in his role as timekeeper, studied his watch as Hughes cajoled and slapped his fighter back to consciousness. The crowd was silent, shocked at what they had witnessed. Suddenly, the big Dutchman grunted and slowly looked about him.

The timekeeper stepped to the centre of the ring and called for both men to toe the line.

Pablo stepped up and placed his canvas-clad foot on the line, his eyes never leaving Larson as he struggled to his feet. The Dutchman's vision cleared as he stood up. The wet cloth was moved from around his head and Alvin Hughes pushed him forward. Larson's feet steadied as he toed the line. His fists closed as the captain's voice cleared the fog from his brain.

'Fight on.'

Larson moved back and studied the young Mexican before him through glittering, beady eyes. The Dutchman's mouth hung open — to gulp in air — as he realized that he could no longer breathe through his nose, which was trickling blood. The left fist of Ortiz snapped out. The Dutchman ducked and took the blow on his forehead to prevent more damage to his nose. The right cross that followed the left, Larson took on his shoulder. Suddenly, Larson's left arm hooked over the young Mexican's arm, then the Dutchman's knee swung in as he pulled

Ortiz round. Ortiz tried to check his forward momentum but the strength of the Dutchman was too much for him. The young Mexican saw the knee swing forward and instinctively jumped in the air, throwing his legs up behind him, transferring his whole body weight on to his opponent. The Dutchman's knee caught Ortiz in the stomach, but Larson stumbled off-balance and let go of Ortiz who fell to the ground. The Dutchman saw his chance and made to stamp on the fallen youth. Ortiz rolled clear as Larson's foot crashed down, just missing him. Ortiz bounded to his feet and danced away, taking deep breaths as he did so.

Ezra called out a warning to the young Mexican as well as protesting at the behaviour of the Dutchman for trying to maim his young fighter.

The crowd now began to shout as they watched the Dutchman go after Ortiz, but the ring's size was in the young Mexican's favour as he moved quickly out of danger, using every inch of the space available, as he recovered from the knee impact to his stomach.

One or two of the spectators shouted to him to stand and fight as he backed away from the Dutchman, putting the maximum amount of space between them.

Then Ortiz suddenly made his move. He leapt forward, with powerful steps, and bringing up both his feet, smashed them into the huge body of the Dutchman, who was lumbering towards him. Larson shuddered and stopped in his tracks, his face showing shock and pain. Ortiz fell on his back, rolled and bounded up again.

John Ross shouted out, in his excitement, at the Mexican's athleticism. The crowd went wild. Then Ortiz moved in, both fists pounding Larson. The sound of the barrage of punches cracked out. The Dutchman staggered back, his legs seemingly treading fresh air as his senses reeled. When the barrage momentarily stopped, Larson stood swaying, his mouth agape, gasping for air, watching

Ortiz as if in a dream.

Alvin Hughes stood up, shouting abuse at Ortiz about using his feet. Those close to him, who had bet on the Mexican, told him in no uncertain manner to shut up as it was the Dutchman who had used his knees first. Ezra muttered anxiously under his breath that it was no time to be stoppin' and gawkin'. He need not have worried.

Larson staggered forward as the young Mexican danced backwards, from side to side. The Dutchman's vision was blurring as he tried to concentrate on his elusive opponent. Ortiz danced within range before darting backwards and the Dutchman mustered all his strength to swing a mighty punch that travelled through thin air. The power of it overbalanced him and he fell to his knees. Only his will power and brute determination stopped him from keeling over.

Now the young Mexican moved in. Larson reached out blindly to grab his tormentor. Ortiz stood perfectly balanced evading the clutching hands as he drove home expert punches with both fists. He turned from the waist, body swivelling, his whole weight and strength behind each blow. The features of the Dutchman were changed by the cuts that opened up as the bare knuckles struck home. Suddenly the Dutchman fell forward and lay still.

A sudden silence came over the crowded building. Pablo Ortiz stood over his opponent; his chest heaving; his fists bloodied. Captain Turner entered the ring and signalled Ortiz to move away from the prostrate body. The captain took out his timepiece and the crowd remained silent as the seconds ticked away. Alvin Hughes struggled to turn the heavy prostrate form of his fighter over and, wiping the blood from his fighter's face, tried to revive him. Larson lay still, his breathing irregular and shallow. The minute over, Captain Turner called out for the contestants to toe the line but Larson was past hearing.

After first calling for the town doctor, Captain Turner raised the hand of Pablo Ortiz and proclaimed him the winner.

Voices were now raised as John Ross stood up to accept the congratulations of his friends and backers. Ezra ducked under the rope to drape a coat round the shoulders of the young Mexican.

'You sure are some mean fighter,' he choked, with tears of joy in his eyes, as he handed young Pablo a cloth to wipe the sweat from his face. His big arms wrapped round Ortiz, hugging him. They were soon joined by Lee Brent, who managed to fight his way through the excited crowd to stand beside his young Mexican friend to offer his congratulations.

'You're a rich man now, Pablo. We've won a lot of money tonight. You get equal share. You won't have to fight ever again unless you want to.'

The town doctor was working on

Larson, in his corner, where he had been unceremoniously dragged by Hughes and Brock. The rancher stood silently alongside as slowly his fighter stirred and opened his eyes.

The doctor gave a sigh, 'You had me worried for a minute,' he told Larson as the Dutchman slowly got to his feet supported by Brock and Hughes.

John Ross had, by now, joined Ortiz and, patting him on the shoulder, he said, 'You did well.'

'Thank you, Señor Ross. Now I will remind you of your promise: did you not say that I can have anything if I win?'

The plantation owner raised his eyebrows and shook his head in surprise at the question.

'You have not forgotten, Señor Ross?'

'No. No lad, I have not forgotten. We can talk about it later.' John Ross was not a man to go back on his word. 'For the moment, I have more urgent business with Alvin Hughes, there.'

The plantation owner crossed the ring to where the rancher was attending to Larson. Hughes turned to face the plantation owner as he heard Ross say, 'It was a good fight, Alvin.'

He greeted Ross with a limp handshake, saying, 'Your Mex used some tactics that I didn't approve of.' Ross shrugged. 'It's all in the game, Alvin. Your man's been known to use indiscreet tactics. Oh, by the way, did you know somebody tried to kill my fighter?' John Ross studied the man before him for any sign of surprise.

'You're not trying to say it was me who tried to shoot the Mex, are you?'

'No,' said the plantation owner. 'And, by the way, I didn't say he was shot at.'

Ross turned away from the rancher, catching Brock's eye as he did so. Brock's hatred was evident in his stare. John Ross nodded to the gunman.

So it was Hughes who was responsible for the attempted killing. John Ross knitted his brows in thought. It had been Hughes who had insisted on adding the clause on the betting about either of the fighters not turning up. But would the rancher have gone so far as to try and kill Ortiz?

John Ross decided he would and Brock was just the man to do the killing. Further thought on the matter was interrupted by his friends as he returned to their company. The night went well. Captain Turner and his ladies were in fine form and the food and drink were plentiful and appetizing. Hughes left the celebration early, choosing not to stay aboard the paddle-steamer, which was unusual for him.

★ ★ ★

Pablo Ortiz could not wait for the next day to arrive. Lee Brent had told him that his share of the money would be put in the bank. John Ross, true to his word, had offered him a choice of two horses from his fine stable.

Pablo Ortiz lay in bed that night,

dreaming of his future. He would go back to his homeland with horses of good pedigree. He would buy a *hacienda*, have his own *remuda* of fine horses but first he would avenge the death of Pedro Gomez. Don Felipe would be made to pay for that, and his lying daughter. Pablo finally fell asleep, to dream of whipping Don Felipe from the back of a thoroughbred while his daughter watched the Lopez *hacienda* being destroyed by flames.

The sounds from the stable below echoed up the stairs to his room. He rose quickly and dressed, wincing with surprise to find his knuckles raw and stiff. He picked up the coffee pot which was still warm. Ezra had topped it up and left it for him. He poured a cup and stood sipping at the brown liquid, the events of the previous evening still fresh in his mind.

His fight with the big Dutchman had surprised the spectators. The young Mexican smiled at himself in the broken mirror. He, Pablo Ortiz, had done well since he had left Mexico. Today he would sit down and talk to his friend, Lee Brent, to see how much he had in the bank, then he would see Señor Ross about the horses.

The footsteps climbing the stairs broke into his thoughts. Ezra entered the room, his white teeth shining in his smiling face. 'You sure can sleep some, Mr Champion. Do you want I cook you some breakfast?'

'No, thank you, Señor Ezra. I am too excited to eat,' replied Ortiz, as he put down the empty cup.

The big hands of Ezra gently clasped the shoulders of the young Mexican. 'You did well, last night, boy. You sure surprised folks from round these parts. Yes sir, especially Mr Ranchowner and that there Dutchman.' Ezra's smile broadened as he relived the previous evening's exploits, shadowboxing the young man's attacks as if they had been his. The smile faded when Pablo Ortiz got out his bag and began to pack his clothes into it.

'What are you doin', boy?' he asked, as he watched the young Mexican retrieve the .45 pistol he had stowed away so many months ago. Pablo checked it and put it into his waistband.

'I'll be leaving today, Ezra,' he told the big Negro, 'as soon as I settle with Señor Brent and Señor Ross. Then I am going back to Mexico to see Don Felipe, the man responsible for Pedro's death. I will challenge him and kill him.'

The young Mexican's hand streaked across his body and before Ezra could blink he was staring down the barrel of the Colt .45. Ortiz laughed at the look of amazement on Ezra's face. He replaced the gun into his waistband. 'I am what you would say fast on the draw, yes?' Ezra nodded. Pablo left the bemused Negro standing by the bed, staring at the packed bag.

Ortiz went downstairs, through the stables and approached the big house. He had a lot to talk about with both John Ross and Lee Brent. Pablo knocked on the door to be answered by Maisie, the house-keeper.

'I have come to see Señor Ross and Señor Brent,' he told the young Negress who, this morning, had a more welcoming look on her face. It was evident that she had heard what had happened the previous night and that now the young Mexican was to be seen in a new light. She let him into the house, not leaving him standing on the veranda as would have been usual.

'Stand there. I will go and call Mr Brent.' she said. She was back in no time with a message from the gambler for him to wait on the veranda, with perhaps a cup of coffee and a biscuit, the housekeeper suggested. Ortiz nodded and ambled outside to sit and wait.

The Mexican was finishing his refreshments when the gambler appeared. Lee Brent was smiling and happy. He had had a good night both on shore and on the *Mississippi Queen*. His gambling had paid high dividends both on his fighter and later at the card table.

'Are you OK?' he enquired of his young friend.

'*Si*, señor. I am very well,' Pablo replied standing up to shake hands.

Brent noticed the gun in Ortiz's waistband. Seeing the gambler's enquiring glance, Ortiz told his friend that it was time for him to be moving on. Today if possible.

'Why don't you stay here? John Ross would like you to stay on as his wrangler. Also he would like you to continue fighting for him,' the gambler countered.

Pablo Ortiz listened to Lee Brent, before shaking his head, in reply.

'I must return to my homeland. You know why, *señor*.

Lee Brent nodded in agreement. Deep down he always knew that one day the young Mexican would return to confront his *ex-patron*.

'I'll come with you,' Lee Brent offered. 'Don Felipe has already tried to kill you. In Mexico his word carries a lot of weight and authority. I have over twenty thousand dollars here for you. Won't that keep you here?'

Pablo Ortiz crumpled in the chair, and lowered his head, 'You have been a good friend to me and you have always given me good advice but I must go, Señor Brent.'

'I know. Just thought I'd try to dissuade you. You're a good source of income to me, Pablo Ortiz.'

They both grinned at one another before Brent continued, 'We'll take a trip into town and get most of your money settled in the bank. John Ross will have some horses for you to check over this afternoon. He says you can take your pick, excepting King Cotton.'

'That is good, *señor*. I will need some money for what I have to do, but I will not need the horses. I will come back for them. First I must settle my account with Don Felipe.' He paused for a while, looking deep into his friend's eyes. 'If things go wrong, tell Señor Ross he can keep the horses.' His voice thickened and he struggled to clear his throat. '*Adios, amigo.*'

'*Vaya con Dios,*' Brent murmured as they shook hands, knowing that soon both would go their separate ways.

12

John Ross and the gambler stood on the veranda watching Pablo Ortiz ride off in the direction of Rossville. The young Mexican had refused Brent's offer to accompany him as far as the town where he intended to purchase a new saddle, new clothes and a supply of bullets for the .45 that nestled in his waist-band.

Brent sighed and shook his head. 'He'd have done better staying put instead of galloping back to Mexico to confront Don Felipe and that daughter of his. Mind, the shooting of Pedro Gomez sure fired him up again. He blames Don Felipe for that.'

John Ross turned to Lee Brent. 'I don't think the Mexican don was responsible.'

The gambler frowned. 'Who else do you think it could have been?'

'I have a feeling that it could have been Hughes's man, Brock,' Ross said, and went on to tell Brent about his conversation with Hughes at the fight. The gambler was surprised by what he heard but could see the point of the plantation-owner's reasoning.

'Hughes is a sidewinder. That's all I can say,' added John Ross. The old man's observations gave Brent room for thought. He wished he had had this conversation before his young friend had left.

A week later, the gambler sat in the town saloon, studying his cards, but his mind was not totally on the game. He looked up at the three players who occupied the table with him.

'I'll take one,' he said, tossing a card from his hand. Picking up the one offered in exchange and seeing that it was no better than the one he had tossed in, he threw the hand on to the table.

Jed Pringle, the storekeeper, who was dealing, looked at the other two poker players. Both tossed their hands in. Pringle sighed. He'd expected more from the hand he had but it looked like his winnings were going to be small tonight.

'What's wrong with you these days, Brent? You don't seem interested in the game,' Pringle said, picking up the meagre pot. Brent gave Pringle a wry smile.

'My mind's elsewhere,' he said, scooping up the remainder of his money. 'I'll call it a night, gentlemen, and make way for someone else.' As he made to rise, he saw Alvin Hughes enter the saloon, with Brock, as usual, in his wake. The rancher had not been seen in town since Ortiz defeated his fighter.

'You're not leaving this early, are you, Brent?' Hughes commented, as he strode over to the table. 'Have you cleaned them out already?' he smirked, indicating Pringle and the other two card players.

'His luck's out,' Pringle said, as

he idly shuffled the cards in front of him.

'So, I'm not interrupting anything, then. How's your Mex friend? I was wondering if he'd fight the Dutchman again but this time on board the *Mississippi Queen* where he can't run away.'

Brent ignored the rancher as he pocketed his money and straightened himself up.

'Mr Hughes asked you a question. Where's the greaser?' Brock stepped in front of Lee Brent, his hand close to the gun on his hip. The gambler took a step back, his right hand sliding up to his jacket lapel, ready to reach inside for the gun nestling in his shoulder holster.

Alvin Hughes studied the gambler. It was obvious by his manner that he had confidence in his ability to get to the gun that was concealed under his jacket. Hughes knew Brock's capabilities, but the gambler was an unknown quantity.

'Let's not cause any trouble with our gambling friend,' Hughes said, addressing Brock. 'We'll call on John Ross to arrange another fight with the Mex.'

Lee Brent relaxed. As he did so, Brock's hand pulled the big .45 from its holster at a signalling nod from the rancher. Too late, the gambler realized he had been hoodwinked. Hughes had caused a distraction with his conversation, giving his gunny the edge. Brent darted his hand inside his jacket and managed to pull his gun free of its holster as Brock fired. The gambler fell backwards and his gun slid from his fingers with a clatter. It all happened so quickly that the watching card players and drinkers were taken by surprise. All Lee Brent could feel was a burning in his gut as he lay on the saloon floor. He heard Alvin Hughes say something about the gambler going for his gun first, then Pringle's voice shouting for someone to get the doctor as the storekeeper's face blurred before him and he floated off in a red mist of pain.

Alvin Hughes felt a degree of satisfaction, as he and Brock left the saloon. The rancher had lost a lot of money to the gambler as well as to his old adversary, John Ross, and it was Brent who had brought the Mex to Rossville. Now, he, Hughes, had paid him back in his own way.

The town doctor knelt beside Lee Brent. Pringle had stemmed the flow of blood while waiting for the doctor to arrive. Between them, they began to remove the clothing from around Brent's wound. Around the gambler's waist was a well-packed money-belt. A bullet hole had been burnt neatly through the belt and the thick wad of notes it contained.

'I've seen some strokes of luck in my time . . . ' the doctor began, shaking his head in amazement. 'Get him upstairs into a spare room. I think he'll live.'

The doctor followed the men carrying

Brent. He eyed the gambler's money-belt as he washed his hands. He knew one thing: for the work he had to do on Brent he would be well paid.

Once the wounded man was settled comfortably the doctor prepared to leave.

'You're a lucky young man,' he told Lee Brent. 'The fruits of your labour saved your life. I don't think the slug went far enough in to do too much damage but you'll need to rest up till that wound heals.'

Lee Brent lay in the bed in the saloon for a week before moving back to the Ross plantation to recover completely.

★ ★ ★

In the meantime, Pablo Ortiz had made his way to Mexico to confront Don Felipe about the shooting of Pedro Gomez. He was hardly recognizable as the same young, subservient boy he had been when he had left Mexico. Now he was a man of means, not the *remudero* who had run bleeding and whipped into the night.

He slowed his horse to a walk and rode erect and confident to the crest of a rise which gave him a grand view of his *ex-patron*'s *hacienda*, which lay spread before him in the valley below. As he urged his horse forward he suppressed feelings of foreboding. His honour and the revenge of his old *caporal* were at stake. He patted the concho that lay in his breast pocket. Today he would confront and challenge Don Felipe Lopez and God would be the judge.

Crossing the valley, he studied the vast layout of buildings that comprised his ex-*patron*'s *hacienda*. Reining in for a second, he checked his handgun before replacing it in his waistband.

Taking a deep breath, he touched his tiring horse forward for the last half-mile of the journey. As he neared the main buildings, he passed a few familiar workers but ignored their stares. His horse's hooves slowly clattered across the paved area in front of the main building and the door opened to reveal Don Felipe framed in the doorway. He watched the young man as he came to halt before him.

'What do you want?' There was no welcome in the voice of the *hacendado* and no sign of fear as he watched Pablo adjust the gun in his waistband.

'I see you are carrying a gun. Have you killing on your mind?'

'It is you who is the killer. I have come to avenge the death of Pedro Gomez,' Ortiz said.

Don Felipe seemed taken aback at the accusation Pablo was directing at him.

A number of the *hacendado*'s workers appeared silently from nearby buildings and stood in a semicircle behind the mounted visitor. A few of them sported weapons to combat any threat Pablo Ortiz might present to their *patron*. The don waved them away and turned his attention to Ortiz.

'Get down from your horse and

come into the house. You, Miguel, take the animal and look after it,' he called to one of the workers.

Ortiz dismounted and let Miguel take his horse. He walked towards the front door and cautiously followed his ex-*patron* into the *hacienda*. Pablo gazed round at the splendour of the room he had entered. He had never seen inside the main building all the time he had worked there. Don Felipe stood by the large fireplace. There was no sign of his daughter.

'What is this you accuse me of? The killing of Pedro Gomez?'

Ortiz snorted in defiance. No longer in awe of his ex-*patron*, he recounted in detail the events of the day when Pedro had met his death.

'And you thought it was I who was responsible for this?' the don asked.

'Yes. You threatened me and Pedro at the race meeting,' Ortiz reminded him in rising tones, his hand close to his waistband.

At the sound of the young Mexican's

raised voice, the housekeeper came from the back of the house. She stepped nervously inside the room and asked Don Felipe if he wanted anything. The don dismissed her with a wave of his hand. When she left, he turned to Pablo Ortiz and with a sigh indicated that they be seated. Pablo shook his head and stood alert and angry as the *hacendado* turned his back on him and settled himself in a large armchair.

'This is very difficult for me,' Don Felipe began. 'I expected you to return one day but not to accuse me of murder. That I made a wrong judgement against you, yes, that is what I was expecting you to accuse me of.'

'You did, you did. That too . . . Ortiz interrupted.

'Do you think you would be alive if I still believed that you had dishonoured my daughter?'

The truth of the don's words crowded out Pablo's protests. He stood open-mouthed as the *hacendado* continued, in halting tones. 'After our confrontation at the race meeting, my daughter — in her distress — told me what had really happened. The truth hurt my pride and that of my family name. In punishment I have sent her away and have waited for this day to come.'

He studied the young Mexican. Pablo's face registered surprise at the words of Don Felipe. He was confused now. If the don's daughter had confessed, there had been no need for him to kill Pedro or himself.

Ortiz dug into his pocket and took out the silver concho he had found where the bushwhacker had lain in wait. The young Mexican handed it to Don Felipe who, after studying it, passed it back.

'Is that what made you believe I was responsible for Pedro's death? Anybody can buy those anywhere. Many people witnessed our encounter at the race meeting and heard the threats made. Perhaps you should look closer to home. Who would have benefited by his or your death?'

This statement set Pablo Ortiz thinking. He was surprised at what the don had said. He shook his head in bewilderment and at the don's second behest sat down to ponder, in confusion, the facts that had now been revealed to him.

Don Felipe could see that he had given his young visitor something to think about with regards to the shooting of Gomez.

'As for the incident with my daughter,' the *hacendado* continued with some difficulty, 'if you wish, I will publicly state your innocence, for you to hear, though all who work here know the reason I have sent her away.'

Pablo Ortiz stood up and, straightening his shoulders, stepped formally across the room to stand before the seated don.

'You have cleared my name to all that knew me, Don Felipe. Our vendetta is ended,' the young Mexican stated.

The *hacendado* nodded solemnly.

'The hospitality of my home is at your disposal, Señor Ortiz.'

Pablo Ortiz knew then that he had been truly vindicated.

Now he had to return to the Ross plantation and talk to Lee Brent and John Ross. Perhaps, with their help, he could find out who had been responsible for Pedro Gomez's death.

That night, the young Mexican chose to sleep in the servants' quarters and the next day he rode away from the *hacienda* and did not look back.

13

The young Mexican did not go directly back to the plantation. Instead he made a detour and took the ferry across the Rio Grande and made his way to Tucson. He would deal with the problem of Pedro's death later, for now he had more urgent things on his mind. It was time for him to think of settling down with a good woman. He had the money to buy a home, now he needed to choose a wife to look after it and himself, as he worked to make himself rich, breeding horses.

If Katherine, the young waitress he had met in Ryan's Café, in Tucson, was still free, he was in a position to offer her marriage.

Ortiz rode slowly past the sheriff's office in Tucson. He met the stare of Ed Stewart, the town marshal, nodded and rode past to the Ryan Café that still displayed the notice, 'Try our Irish stew. The best in town'. Ortiz dismounted and smiled to himself as he heard footsteps hurrying in his direction from the lawman's office. Ed Stewart caught him up as he entered the café.

'What do you want here?' the marshal asked, taking hold of Pablo's elbow and steering him towards an empty table. 'What's brought you back to town?'

Before Ortiz could answer, a familiar voice shyly intoned, 'Hello, handsome,' and he found himself looking into the smiling, if slightly anxious, face of Katherine, the waitress.

'Everything is the same. The good smell of food and you, *señorita*. It is *señorita* is it not?' Pablo remarked. Katherine flushed and nodded.

'Never mind that,' Ed Stewart interrupted. 'Get us some coffee, for now, Katherine, and leave us alone. We've some talking to do.'

The Irishwoman behind the counter frowned across as Katherine put in her order. She caught sight of Ortiz and the marshal and recognized the young Mexican as the fist-fighter who had beaten her husband, Pat Ryan. The Irishman had made a complete recovery, but there was still some ill-feeling towards the Mexican for the way the fight had ended.

Ed Stewart was aware that the fight had ended. Ryan and Ortiz was still talked about in the town and a lot of money had been lost by disgruntled punters. The marshal did not want trouble flaring up should somebody in the town decide to get satisfaction by killing the young Mexican.

'Why have you come back here? And where's the gambler?'

'My good friend is in Rossville, Señor Marshal, and the reason I am back here is to ask the *señorita* to marry me.'

Ed Stewart looked at the Mexican in amazement. 'Who? Katherine? What makes you think she'll marry you, a fist-fighter and a Mexican at that?'

Pablo's face fell. He realized that

although Ed Stewart's retort was blunt it was likely true. However he would not let himself be put off.

'I would make her a good husband, Señor Marshal. I have money enough to buy a home and I promise that I will treat her well, if she will agree to marry with me. That is all I am here for. If she does not want this, I will go.'

Katherine returned with their coffee and placed it on the table. 'I'm sorry,' she said, addressing Pablo, with a forlorn look on her face, 'but Mrs Ryan says you'll have to go when you've had your coffee.'

'Don't you want to know why he is here?' Ed Stewart asked the pretty waitress.

'I'm sure it's none of my business.'

'It just might be: he wants to marry you.'

Katherine's eyes widened in surprise. She glanced quickly from the marshal to Ortiz and then towards Mrs Ryan, who was standing, arms akimbo, scowling over in their direction. Turning back

238

to fix the young Mexican with a steady gaze, she asked in low tones, 'And what have you to say for yourself, Mister handsome fist-fighter?'

Pablo Ortiz had watched Katherine's reaction to the marshal's words. Her initial surprise was soon controlled and nothing in her manner told him what she was thinking.

'Señor Marshal is right. I, Pablo Ortiz, come to ask you to marry with me. I am a Mexican. This might not be to your liking, but you should know I am a man of honour. I do not come with empty hands. I have much money and much plans. If you will marry with me, we will share a good life with a house and land and horses . . . '

'Stop right there, young man, or you'll have me acceptin' your offer.' Ed Stewart interrupted.

Pablo Ortiz nodded and went silent. Both men gazed expectantly at Katherine.

'Drink your coffee,' she said, adding, 'but take your time,' as she left the table and went over to Mrs Ryan, who stood patiently listening as a slightly flushed Katherine told her why the young Mexican had returned to Tucson.

The café owner allowed Katherine to finish before making comment.

'What in the name of all that's holy are you thinking of, Katherine? Have we not taken good care of you; given you a good home? Your bed is comfortable, is it not? Your belly's full, is it not? What more can a girl want?'

'That handsome Mexican,' declared Katherine, with deep conviction. Mrs Ryan looked in Pablo's direction. She had to admit that he was very handsome — nearly as handsome as an Irishman — and better dressed and more confident than when she had last seen him.

'Well, you're old enough to know your own mind and sure enough you're more than ready to wed. Go your own way, Katherine, for I can see no words of mine will stop you,' she told the young waitress, who immediately returned to the table.

'That's settled then, Señor Pablo Ortiz. I will marry you.'

Ed Stewart nearly fell off his chair. The Mexican stood up and, with a big grin, bowed low over the extended hand of his future bride.

'Now, Señor Marshal, if you will oblige, I shall leave Señorita Katherine in your care till I return.'

'Hold your horses, young man. If I am to be responsible for this young lady, there's a few things we need to discuss,' Ed Stewart blustered.

'Oh, that's all right, Marshal. I can stay on here till Pablo gets back and if there's any need, I know where to find you,' Katherine giggled.

'Right then, I'll leave you two to talk, but remember, young man, it might not be too healthy for you to make your stay overlong.'

The marshal stopped at the counter to exchange bewilderments with Mrs Ryan before leaving the café.

Pablo and Katherine sat for a while discussing their future before Pablo stood up to take his leave.

'I go now, for I have much to do. I give my word that I will be back soon to make you my wife.'

Pablo Ortiz bowed low over her hand once more and left the café.

'Well, I'll be darned' murmured Ed Stewart, as later, he watched the young Mexican ride out of town.

* * *

It was nearly a fortnight since Lee Brent had been shot. He was still confined to bed but with the care and attention of Maya and her potions, he was recovering fast. He woke early in the morning and lay waiting for the old woman's visit. Today he felt stronger and clearer headed. His fingers felt the tender area under the bandage. His money-belt had certainly saved his life. Brent eased back the covers and was trying to get out of the bed when

242

old Maya entered his room.

'You goin' somewhere, Mr gamblin'-man? Not yet a while, I say,' she said, pulling away the bed clothes and signalling him to lie flat. He succumbed to her examination and treatment of the healing wound.

'Reckon I'm well enough to get up today, Maya. What do you think?' Brent asked, as she wrapped a clean bandage around his waist.

'I think . . . ' she said, and prodded the area over his wound, causing him to inhale quickly. 'Ah,' Maya commented in a satisfactory tone, 'maybe for a little while. I see Master John.'

The gambler watched while the old woman prepared a medicinal drink. He grimaced as he sipped the foul-tasting grey concoction.

'I leave now,' the old woman said. 'Today, you walk a bit.' Maya collected her basket and hesitated at the door. 'Ezra say your friend is back.'

As she left, Maisie entered carrying a breakfast tray.

'She said, Pablo's back, Maisie. Is it true?' Lee Brent grunted as he tried to struggle to his feet.

Maisie downed the tray and clucked like an old hen. 'I think you should stay abed, Mr Brent. Master John tell me nothin' about you being on your feet.'

'I'll sit at the table, Maisie. Maya said it's OK to walk about.'

'That ol' witch woman is not my boss, Mr Brent. I do as Master John say. He say . . .'

'I'll settle it with Mr Ross, Maisie,' Brent interrupted. 'Go and see Ezra. Ask him if it's true that Pablo's back.'

The housekeeper hurried away as Brent reached for his clothes nearby. He winced at the pain. He was dressed and fed when Maisie returned.

'The young Mexican is back and he'll be over to see you soon as Ezra wakes him,' she told Lee Brent, as she helped him out onto the veranda to sit and wait for his friend.

He did not have to wait long before

he saw Ortiz hurrying towards him. Ezra had already told Pablo about Brent being shot. Ortiz climbed the few steps of the veranda, urgent questions on his lips.

'Whoa, slow down, Pablo. I'm doing fine. And you? You don't look as if you've been badly done by. What happened in Mexico?'

It did not take Pablo long to go over the events from Don Felipe's revelation about his daughter and his denial concerning the death of Pedro Gomez to his proposal of marriage to the pretty young waitress, Katherine.

'But first I have to avenge my old *caporal*'s death.' Pablo concluded.

'Well, you certainly have been busy since I last set eyes on you. It's good to have you back, my young friend. Old John Ross and I got talking after you left; he don't think the don was responsible for Pedro's death either.'

'Don Felipe said I should look closer to home. He asked me who else knew of the trouble at the race meeting.'

Lee Brent winced as he moved to get more comfortable before he settled down to tell Ortiz of the old plantation-owner's suspicions concerning Alvin Hughes and about the shooting of himself by Brock in the saloon.

At that moment, John Ross and his son joined them on the veranda. Pablo stood up and acknowledged the plantation owner.

'It's good to see you Pablo,' John Ross said warmly. 'And all in one piece.'

Turning to Brent he said, 'And you're looking better. Maya has done a good job on you.'

'Pablo's come back with an apology of sorts from Don Felipe, but he strongly denies having anything to do with Pedro's death. Looks like you were right in thinking it was Alvin Hughes's gunny, Brock, who did it.'

'I will go and face this Señor Brock,' Pablo said, moving away and heading for the steps.

'Wait.' Lee Brent struggled to rise.

'Let me get my gun. I'll come with you.'

'No, you stay here.' It was Daniel Ross who spoke. 'I'll go with Pablo, Pa, and see he gets a fair crack at Brock. That sidewinder Hughes has gone too far this time and if he pokes his nose in, I'll shoot it off.'

Lee Brent had to admit he would be more of a hindrance than a help. He had heard talk about Daniel Ross being good with a gun; he just hoped, for his friend's sake, it was true.

Pablo Ortiz hurried away to get his pistol. Daniel Ross went into the house and returned with his belt and holster round his waist. He was checking the rounds in his gun when Ezra came from the stables with the young Mexican. Seeing Ezra, John Ross called to him to get the buckboard ready, declaring, 'I'm going along, too.'

Lee Brent struggled to his feet.

'If you're all going, I'm coming as well,' he said.

The journey to the Rolling H was

bone-shaking for Lee Brent, who sat alongside the plantation owner, trying not to wince at every jolt the buckboard made. Pablo sat up front with Ezra and Daniel Ross. They slowed down as they entered the ranch yard.

Jake, Hughes's wrangler, hearing their approach, laid down the hammer he was using to beat a piece of steel into shape on the anvil, and popped his head out of the farrier's door. Recognizing the now stationary carriage, he spat out and ambled over.

'Howdy, Mr Ross.' he called.

Daniel acknowledged the welcome. 'Is Hughes about?'

The man nodded in reply 'He went into the barn for something. You want I go get him?' He squinted at the loaded carriage.

'If you will,' John Ross answered him, as he climbed out of the carriage to join his son and the young Mexican in the yard.

Jake ambled over to the barn. Alvin Hughes came out at his call. Brock, as usual, was close at hand. He was surprised to see the number of callers.

'What do they want,' Brock muttered.

'Probably to take up the challenge to fight Larson on the boat. They've got the Mex with them.'

They strolled over to the buckboard and Brock was surprised to see that Daniel Ross was armed.

'Well, John, have you decided to give us a return match on the steamer, with your fighter here?' the rancher asked.

'As a matter of fact I haven't anything to say, Hughes. The Mexican has something to ask you and as it's to do with something that happened on our land, Daniel and I came along to see he gets a square deal, not like Brent here.'

Alvin Hughes shifted uneasily. Old Jake, the wrangler-cum-blacksmith, quietly stepped back a pace or two into the barn, where he could safely listen and watch. Sensing the hostility of the visitors, Brock's hand nestled by his holster.

'And what does the Mex have to say?' Hughes asked

'He thinks it was Brock here who tried to kill him and shot his friend instead. He wants to face Brock now,' John Ross said.

The ranch owner laughed. 'Brock's not a fighter . . .'

Pablo Ortiz butted in. 'This Brock is a killer who shot my friend in the back. I will fight him with a gun, face to face.'

Brock pushed Hughes to one side. 'What he says is lies. I didn't shoot no greaser and if he wants to take a chance against me, he can try.'

Alvin Hughes held up his hand for silence and looked about nervously. He spotted Jake in the barn doorway but the rest of his crew were working the cattle out on the range. Not that any of them were any good with a gun. Hughes tried to get the group's attention away from Brock.

'What happens if Brock kills the Mex?' he roared, stepping backwards, but no one paid him any notice. Brock's hand streaked to his gun. The Mexican moved quicker. Pablo's hand flew across his body and he drew and fired all in one movement. His slug hit Brock in the chest, knocking him to the ground. The rancher stood watching in disbelief as Brock's feet beat a death tattoo on the ground. Daniel Ross drew his gun as the rancher made a move for his. Hughes stopped. His shoulders sagged.

'Well, Hughes, do you fancy a second chance?' Daniel Ross said, replacing his gun and squaring up to the rancher. Alvin Hughes shook his head. Old Jake stood watching and waiting to see what happened next. It was John Ross who spoke.

'If I was you, Hughes, I'd bury Brock and get out. It's a pity I can't prove it was your orders that killed Pablo's friend. If I could, I'd see you hang. All I know for sure is that no Mexican was responsible for the plantation killing. Doesn't take much to work out who else it might be. Jake here is witness to fair play today, which is more than can be said of you and your gunny. The best thing would be for you to sell up and leave. You won't be welcome around Rossville anymore.'

Within weeks, the Rolling H ranch was sold and the new owners, Lee Brent and Pablo Ortiz, renamed it the Silver Concho, Lee Brent left the running of the ranch to his Mexican friend and his wife, Katherine, whilst he rode the paddle-steamers, doing what he did best, winning money.

THE END

We do hope that you have enjoyed reading this large print book.

Did you know that all of our titles are available for purchase?

We publish a wide range of high quality large print books including:
Romances, Mysteries, Classics, General Fiction, Non Fiction and Westerns.

Special interest titles available in large print are:
The Little Oxford Dictionary Music Book, Song Book Hymn Book, Service Book

Also available from us courtesy of Oxford University Press:
Young Readers' Dictionary (large print edition) Young Readers' Thesaurus (large print edition)

For further information or a free brochure, please contact us at:
Ulverscroft Large Print Books Ltd., The Green, Bradgate Road, Anstey, Leicester, LE7 7FU, England. Tel: (00 44) **0116 236 4325 Fax:** (00 44) **0116 234 0205**

Other titles in the
Linford Western Library:

RIO REPRISAL

Jake Douglas

Life had taken on a new meaning for Jordan and all he wanted was to be left alone, but it was not to be. Back home, there were only blackened ruins and Mandy had been taken by the feared Apache, Wolf Taker. The only men Jordan could turn to for help were the outlaws with whom he had once ridden, but their price was high and bloody. Nevertheless, Jordan was prepared to tear the entire southwest apart as long as he found Mandy.

DEATH MARCH IN MONTANA

Bill Foord

Held under armed guard in a Union prison camp, Captain Pat Quaid learns that the beautiful wife of the sadistic commandant wants her husband killed. She engineers the escape of Quaid and his young friend Billy Childs in exchange for Quaid's promise to turn hired gunman. He has reasons enough to carry out the promise, but he's never shot a man in cold blood. Can he do it for revenge, hatred or love?

A LAND TO DIE FOR

Tyler Hatch

There were two big ranches in the valley: Box T and Flag. Ben Tanner's Box T was the larger and he ran things his way. Wes Flag seemed content to play second fiddle to Tanner — until he married Shirley. But the trouble hit the valley and soon everyone was involved. Now it was all down to Tanner's loyal ramrod, Jesse McCord. He had to face some tough decisions if he was to bring peace to the troubled range — and come out alive.

THE SAN PEDRO RING

Elliot Conway

US Marshal Luther Killeen is working undercover as a Texan pistolero in Tucson to find proof that the San Pedro Ring, an Arizona trading and freighting business concern, is supplying arms to the bronco Apache in the territory. But the fat is truly in the fire when his real identity is discovered. Clelland Singer, the ruthless boss of the Ring, hires a professional killer, part-Sioux Louis Merlain, to hunt down Luther. Now it is a case of kill or be killed.

GOING STRAIGHT IN FRISBEE

Marshall Grover

Max and Newt were small-time thieves, a couple of unknowns, until the crazy accident that won them a reputation and a chance to reform. But going straight in a town like Frisbee was not so easy. Two tough Texans were wise to them and, when gold was discovered in that region, Frisbee boomed and a rogue-pack moved in to prey on prospectors. In the cold light of dawn, the no-accounts marched forth to die.